bitter rose

bitter rose

color me crushed

melody carlson

Th1nk Books
an imprint of NavPress®

© 2006 by Melody Carlson

TH1NK Books is an imprint of NavPress. TH1NK is a registered trademark of NavPress. Absence of * in connection with marks of NavPress or other parties does not indicate an absence of registration of those marks.

ISBN 1-57683-536-7

Cover design by studiogearbox.com
Cover photo by Rubberball
Creative Team: Nicci Jordan, Arvid Wallen, Erin Healy, Cara Iverson, Bob Bubnis

This is a work of fiction. The characters, incidents, and dialogues are products of the author's imagination and are not to be construed as real. Any resemblance to actual events or persons, living or dead, is entirely coincidental.

Published in association with the literary agency of Sara A. Fortenberry.

Carlson, Melody.
   Bitter rose : color me crushed / Melody Carlson.
      p. cm. -- (Truecolors series ; bk. 8)
   Summary: A Mexican-American high school senior deals with the separation and divorce of her parents and their effects on her relationship with them and with God.
   ISBN 1-57683-536-7
   [1. Divorce--Fiction. 2. Mexican Americans--Fiction. 3. Family life--Fiction. 4. Christian life--Fiction.] I. Title.
   PZ7.C216637Bit 2006
   [Fic]--dc22

                              2005021010

Printed in Canada

2 3 4 5 6 7 8 9 10 / 10 09 08 07 06

FOR A FREE CATALOG OF
NAVPRESS BOOKS & BIBLE STUDIES,
CALL 1-800-366-7788 (USA)
OR 1-800-839-4769 (CANADA)

Other Books by Melody Carlson

Blade Silver (NavPress)
Fool's Gold (NavPress)
Burnt Orange (NavPress)
Pitch Black (NavPress)
Torch Red (NavPress)
Deep Green (NavPress)
Dark Blue (NavPress)
DIARY OF A TEENAGE GIRL series (Multnomah)
DEGREES OF GUILT series (Tyndale)
Crystal Lies (WaterBrook)
Finding Alice (WaterBrook)
Looking for Cassandra Jane (Tyndale)

one

LIFE AS I KNOW IT ENDED TODAY. SERIOUSLY, IT'S OVER. NOW, YOU MAY think I'm just being a drama queen, and it wouldn't be the first time I've been accused of blowing something way out of proportion. But, trust me, this is the real deal. It's over.

"What's wrong?" asks my best friend, Claire, when she finally returns my call like two hours later.

"Everything," I tell her. "My life is over."

"What are you talking about, Maggie?"

"It's my parents."

"Are they fighting again?" Her voice sounds bored now and slightly disconnected too, like maybe she's filing her nails, or watching her favorite Home Shopping Network show, or reading her e-mail, or playing a stupid computer game.

"Claire, this is *serious*."

"Oh, Maggie, your parents are constantly fighting. It'll blow over in—"

"No, it's *not* a fight this time. It's over! They are splitting up!"

"Splitting up?" She actually sounds a little shocked. "Really?"

Okay, maybe I've got her attention now. "Yes! Really! My mom just told me. Dad has left."

"No way!"

"Way."

"When did this happen?"

"Last night, apparently. I mean, there I was, going to youth group and spending the night at your house just so they could have some one-on-one time together, as my mom puts it, and then I come home today to discover that it's over. Dad's gone."

"What happened?"

"I'm not really sure. All Mom would tell me is that he's gone and he's not coming back." I start choking up now. "I cannot believe my dad stepped out of my life just like that. I mean, he didn't even have the courtesy to warn me or say good-bye."

"Oh, Maggie, that's too bad. You were one of the few people I know who still had her *original* parents. Your mom and dad actually gave me hope that love might possibly last a lifetime."

"Apparently not."

"So where did your dad go anyway?"

"According to my mom, he's crashing with a friend for the time being. But she also said he's going to get a place of his own before long."

"Did she say why, like what actually brought it to this? Besides all the fighting, I mean."

"No, she wouldn't say anything specific, other than that he left—period. Consequently, we got into this humongous fight. Big surprise. I mean, it's clearly all her fault, Claire. She's driven him away with her constant nagging and complaining and arguing. Honestly, who could stand to live with that woman? I know I can't! I just walked out on her myself. Maybe I'll divorce her too." Yeah, right.

"So where are you now?"

"I'm sitting in my car."

"Where?"

"Outside the mall. I know that's pretty lame, and it's not like I want to go shopping, but I just didn't know where else to go."

"Well, come over here. Nobody's home but me anyway."

"Thanks, Claire." We say good-bye and I immediately turn off my cell phone since I'm sure that Mom will try to call again. She already tried twice while I was waiting for Claire to call back. Fortunately, I have my caller ID and never even picked up. But she did leave a message—a really pathetic one if you ask me.

"Hi, Magdela," she said in this depressed and dreary sounding voice. "I'm so sorry we fought. We really need to talk about this. Please give me a call. I'm worried about you, *mi hija*."

Well, she *should* be worried. It's because of *her* that my life is getting blown to pieces right now. And it's my senior year too—my last year at home before college and the year when you really want the love and support of *both* your parents. My older brother and sister both got that much, but now they're off living their own lives and probably totally oblivious to the fact that our family has completely disintegrated. Like, presto-change-o, *poof!* it's gone. I wonder if my mom has even told them yet. And what about the grandparents? Yeah, I can just imagine how they're going to react.

But here's what really gets me: My parents, the respectable Roberto and Rosa Fernandez, are these born-again Catholic Christians, and they're all into their "reformed" church and their home growth groups and Bible studies, and now *this*? I just don't get it. And they've always told us kids that marriage is a "forever commitment"—that wedding vows are meant to be kept until "death do you part." So what's the deal here? Are they just total hypocrites or what? I have to admit that this disaster even makes me question my own faith. I mean, if this is where it gets you, crud, why bother?

Finally, I'm at Claire's house. She meets me at the door with a big hug. "I'm so sorry, Maggie. I mean, speaking from experience, I know you'll survive it. You *will* get through this. But I know that it totally bites too."

"You got that right."

Claire's parents got divorced when she was only ten. At the time, I was completely shocked and felt so sorry for her and her mom since her dad was pretty much being a jerk. But time passed, and Jeannie eventually remarried this really nice guy named Adam, and I guess I just sort of forgot about Claire's original dad. I think she sort of forgot him too since he pretty much got out of her life. We never even talk about him anymore.

But thinking of this as I follow her into the kitchen doesn't make me feel a bit better. I'm so not ready to have my dad pull a disappearing act on me. The truth is, I really do love my dad—a lot. I mean, I realize he's not perfect, but he's actually pretty cool, for a parent anyway. And I'm a lot closer to him than to my mom. He's the one who usually understands me. I really don't want him to just vanish from my life like Claire's dad did. Maybe it's going to be up to me to hold on to him.

"You know what?" I say as we dig our spoons into a half-full carton of cookie-dough ice cream. "I think maybe I'll live with my dad when he gets his own place."

Her eyebrows lift slightly. "Uh, have you talked to him about this?"

"Of course not. I haven't even seen him since he left home last night. But I'm sure he'll be fine with it. I mean, we've always gotten along a whole lot better than Mom and me. And lately, well, Mom's been pretty witchy to both of us. She's like this devil woman, always on everyone's case. It's like the tiniest things just set her off. You've seen her; she's always grumping about something."

"Yeah, I remember how she came unglued when you forgot the laundry in the washing machine last week."

"Exactly. The woman is totally unreasonable."

"She might be hormonal," suggests Claire with a thoughtful expression. "My mom just warned me that she's starting to go through menopause now and that's going to be worse than PMS." She rolls her eyes. "What fun."

"But your mom's older than mine," I remind her as I scrape my spoon down the side of the carton, getting lots of chocolate this time.

"Well, you never know, Maggie. This thing might blow over— you know, when your parents both come to their senses."

"I don't think that's going to happen. I mean, Mom seemed pretty certain that this is it—that it's over."

Claire licks her spoon and then shakes her head. "I just never figured it would happen to them."

"I'll bet you anything that it was my mom who told him to leave," I say, waving my spoon around for effect. "I can just imagine her going ballistic on him. She probably pointed at the front door and told him to get out and never show his face there again. Maybe she even cussed him out in Spanish."

Claire kind of giggles. "Yeah, I guess I can imagine that too. I mean, I've seen your mom cut loose in *Español* a time or two. It's pretty scary."

"Yeah, and then she freaks if she ever catches me doing the same thing."

"But your dad's so sweet, Maggie. I don't get it. Why would your mom want to throw him out like that?"

"I don't know." I drop my spoon in the carton, blinking back tears. "Well, besides the fact that she's crazy. But seriously, why did she have to go and ruin everything? Why is she so horrible and mean and selfish?" And now the tears are flooding down my cheeks again, and all I can think is that I hate my mom. She makes me sick! And I know I will never, never forgive her for this!

two

A WEEK HAS PASSED, AND ALTHOUGH I'VE LEFT HIM MESSAGES, I STILL haven't seen or spoken to my dad. In fact, I've barely talked to my mom. We both just move silently through the house, making lots of space for each other. The last thing I want is to have an actual conversation with that woman. She tried it a couple of times, and I made it perfectly clear that I have absolutely no interest in speaking to her. I cannot stand her.

It's like she just doesn't care, like she can simply block out the fact that she and Dad have been married for almost twenty-five years. My older sister and brother and I had even started talking about having a big anniversary party for them next April.

"I can't believe it," Elisa said when she called a few days ago. "This is so weird."

"Tell me about it."

"Do you think it's just a passing thing, something they can work out and resolve? Maybe get counseling at church or something?"

I sighed loudly. "I don't know. Mom acts like this is it—like there's absolutely no hope."

"What about Dad?"

"He won't even return my calls."

"Yeah, same here. But that's not like him."

"I think he's really hurting, Elisa," I told her. "I think she broke his heart."

"But *why*?" My usually calm and controlled older sister sounded seriously upset, like this was hitting her as hard as it was hitting me.

"I have no idea."

"Do you think Mom's into another guy?"

I considered this. "I don't know."

"What about that dude she told us about last summer? That new guy at work? What's his name?"

"Mickey?"

"Yeah, I remember her talking about how great Mickey was. She thought he was so brilliant, so good-looking, so full of potential. Don't you remember how she went on and on about him?"

"I thought that was for your sake," I said. "Like she wanted you to hook up with him. Isn't he a little young for Mom?"

"Maybe, but there could be someone else."

"Maybe." But even as I said this, and even as furious as I was at Mom, I had a hard time imagining her getting interested in another guy. It just sounded all wrong.

"You should pop in on her sometime, Maggie—you know, look around the real estate office and see if there's someone who might've turned her head."

"Yeah, right," I told her. "Like I'm going to go in and spy on her."

"Well, it'd be easier for you than me, clear down here in San Diego. Come on, Maggie. Just go look around, okay?"

So I agreed, reluctantly. But I didn't promise to do it right away.

"What about Marc?" Elisa asked. "Has anyone told him yet?"

"I don't know. Mom might've. But she and I aren't really talking much these days."

"Well, maybe you should give him a call, Maggie. Give him a heads-up."

"Why do I get stuck with all this?"

"You're the one at home. You have a better idea of what's going on than we do. I already told you that my conversation with Mom was pretty much useless. She sounded like she was reading from a cue card, almost as if she was drugged or something. She's not taking any meds, is she?"

"I don't know," I said for like the umpteenth time. And that's just how I feel—like I don't know anything.

"Well, check it out, Maggie. Find out what's going on and get back to me. I hate being so far away at times like this, and Marc's going to feel the same way. It's up to you to keep us posted, okay?"

"Yeah," I said without enthusiasm. "I'll see what I can do."

So later that night, I called my brother and actually caught him in his dorm room at the university. And I guess I shouldn't have been too surprised that Marc's take on this was totally different than ours—well, other than the initial shock. I think all three of us felt pretty much the same in that regard.

But after Marc recovered from the bad news, he instantly set his sights on Dad. Of course, I know the reason behind this reaction. I mean, we all know that Marc is Mom's favorite. Oh, she never says as much. No one really does. But Elisa and I both know it's true. And I suppose it's not that unusual in Hispanic households for mothers to be partial to sons—especially *only* sons. I think it goes back to the old days and maintaining the family name and all that crud. Anyway, Marc is indisputably her favorite, and he knows it. It's no surprise that he would defend her. Even so, I found it extremely irritating.

"You know this has to be Dad's fault," Marc said as if he were an expert on marital problems.

"What makes you so sure?"

"It's usually the guy, Maggie. Statistics prove it."

"But Dad's not the typical guy, Marc. For one thing, he's a Christian. And he takes his faith seriously. He even went to that Promise Keepers convention last summer. So it's not really fair to blame him just because he's the guy. How would you like for someone to do that to you?"

"I'm just telling you the statistics, Maggie. Don't shoot the messenger, okay?"

Naturally, that made me feel bad. I mean, between Elisa and Marc, I've probably always been closer to Marc, and I didn't particularly want to take sides against him. But still . . .

"And Dad's a good-looking guy," he told me as if that was a point against him.

"Mom's not exactly ugly," I reminded him.

"But she's Mom," he said in her defense. "Think about it, Maggie."

"But you haven't seen her lately," I said. "She's been a real witch this fall. It's like she's been having some kind of hormonal meltdown or something. Seriously, she's totally impossible. They were fighting all the time."

"That's not all that new."

"And she was swearing at him in Spanish, Marc. Not just once either."

He was quiet for a few moments.

"You can't just automatically blame Dad, Marc—even if you are Mom's favorite."

He didn't even deny that. "Well, why don't you find out what's behind it then, Maggie? Talk to both of them. Get to the bottom of this."

I groaned.

"Come on," he urged. "Just ask some questions and see what's up. And maybe it's not as bad as you think. Maybe it's just a midlife thing, you know, and maybe Dad will buy himself a new car and come home and that'll be it."

"Yeah, maybe so."

"Do you think it might be patched up by Christmas?" he asked hopefully. "I thought maybe I'd bring Liz home to meet everyone."

"Does that mean you guys are getting serious?"

"I wouldn't call it serious. But I thought it might be interesting to see what she thought of our Latino Christmases."

"Well, I have no idea how this thing will be by then. As it is, Thanksgiving isn't looking too great."

"Oh, you never know, Maggie. They could patch it all up by tomorrow. Just give it some time."

"Right."

"And if you find out anything, like what's underneath it all, let me know, okay?"

"Yeah. Just call me Maggie P. I."

He thought that was funny. And by the time we hung up, I thought maybe he was right—that maybe this whole thing was just some kind of midlife fluke that would blow over within the week. But the week has passed, and it appears my parents are still in some kind of standoff.

And then today when I noticed that all photos that included my dad had been removed from the wall along the stairway, I started to get seriously worried. Like, what was up with that? I mean, sure Mom can be furious at Dad if she wants, but does that give her the right to strip him from our entire family? I don't think so.

It's five o'clock on Friday, and Mom still hasn't come home from work. But then she's been working later than usual this week—just one more reason for me to be suspicious that she is up to something. And so I decide to do some snooping around. I suppose I figure that I have the "authority" to do this since both Elisa and Marc insisted I uncover what's going on with our parents. Besides, I want to know what she's done with the family photos. So naturally, my sleuthing begins in my parents' bedroom.

I start on Mom's side, going through the drawers in her bedside table. And, okay, I know this is wrong, and I do feel guilty, but there's something in me that's just compelled, as if I can't help myself. But I don't see anything that looks out of the ordinary. Even her lotion is plain old Jergens like Grandma uses, and the book she's reading—*Reviving Your Marriage* of all things—doesn't really seem to be working for her. After that I go through her bureau drawers, particularly her lingerie drawer, which, according to a magazine article I recently read, could prove to be revealing. But most of the items in there look pretty boring and pathetic, not to mention ancient. Like, does my mom even know that undies come in actual colors these days?

Finally, I go to the big walk-in closet that I tend to envy (since mine is way smaller and packed to overflowing) and am shocked to see that *all* of my dad's things are gone. His side is totally empty—well, other than a couple of lonely dresses that my mom has hung up there to, I'm sure, make herself feel better. But it makes me feel sick. I quickly go through my dad's bureau now and find that it too is empty.

I look at the spot on the wall where my parents' wedding photo used to hang along with the framed wedding announcement. Not only are these pieces gone but the blue wallpaper behind them, which hasn't faded like the rest, is a glaring reminder of what used to hang there. I stand and look around the room and realize that nothing of my dad has been left behind. It's like every single piece of him is gone. Not a trace remains. And it feels as if he's dead—as if my mother murdered him and then neatly disposed of the body.

three

"I THINK I'M GOING TO HAVE TO RETAKE MY SATS," I CONFESS TO CLAIRE as we slowly walk through the mall. We're both sort of glassy-eyed and weary after a long morning of tests. But when we finished, she insisted on coming to a one-day-only shoe sale at Nordstrom's, and I didn't protest.

"Don't worry, Maggie," she assures me. "They say everyone feels like that afterward. It's just part of the letdown after studying so hard and then getting it over with. You just have to let it go."

"But I'm serious," I tell her. "It's like I couldn't focus or concentrate. And I know I totally blew the math."

"I'm sure you did fine. You're always good at tests."

And since I don't want to argue right now, I let it go. Just the same, I'm pretty sure I'll have to retake it. And if Mom gives me a hard time, I'll just tell her that it's her fault. If she hadn't thrown Dad out, I might be in better form. Okay, it probably didn't help that I stayed out a little late last night, but I was so surprised when Brandon Cline asked me out that I totally forgot today's test.

As we enter Nordstrom's, Claire asks me how my date was, as though she's reading my mind.

"Oh, it was okay."

"Just okay?" She turns and looks at me skeptically. "So he's not as hot as you expected?"

I kind of laugh. "No, he's definitely hot. But I'm not so sure he's into me."

"But you said you were out pretty late."

"That's because he didn't call me until seven-thirty, so we ended up going to a movie that started around ten. I didn't get home until after midnight."

"Good thing your dad wasn't home."

I kind of laugh. "Yeah, right." But I was actually thinking it's a small consolation. I honestly think I'd rather have Dad back and get in trouble for breaking my curfew.

"And your mom didn't get on your case?"

"She mentioned the time, like I didn't know. But that was about it."

"Lucky you."

"Right."

"So anyway, do you think he's going to ask you out again?"

"I don't know. Maybe. We ended up playing video games while we waited for the movie, and I think he was pretty surprised when I thoroughly beat him at Penguin Wars."

Claire laughs. "Did you tell him you used to hold the record at the Fifth Street Arcade?"

"Yeah, right. Are you kidding?"

But now we're in the shoe department and Claire immediately goes into her huntress mode. When it comes to shopping, especially for shoes, there's no one quite like Claire. I just have to watch with amazement and admiration. And since I didn't get any allowance this week (thanks to my parents' messed-up lives), I can't really afford to buy anything in here anyway. But I encourage Claire as she tries on dozens of pairs, finally deciding on some black boots that look fantastic on her. Despite myself, I feel a little jealous as we walk out and she's the one carrying a big brown shopping bag.

"So have you talked to your dad yet?" she asks as we head over to the food court.

"He hasn't answered my calls."

"Isn't that kind of weird?"

"Yeah. And I guess I'm getting worried. I even called the friend that he's staying with and left a couple messages."

"Why don't you call him at work?"

"It's an old rule. His boss is a real jerk, and I'm not supposed to bug Dad there unless it's an emergency."

"Oh."

"But I was thinking about stopping by his friend's place," I tell her as we wait in line at Taco Time (my grandma calls these "gringo tacos," but I think they're okay).

"Want to do that on our way home?" she offers.

"Do you mind?"

"Not at all. I think you need to see him."

So after we finish up at the mall, I direct Claire to where my dad's staying. As she drives, I try once again to reach him on his cell, but, as usual, he's not answering.

She pulls up to a slightly run-down apartment complex. I look for the right number and then head over to knock on the door. Fortunately, Claire knows enough to wait in the car. Who knows how this might go? I've only met Dad's friend Chuck once or twice over the years, and I'm not even sure I'll recognize him. But I do know that Chuck got divorced a few years ago. I remember my mom thought it was a shame, and she encouraged my dad to try to talk him into reconciling with his wife. Obviously, that never happened, because when

Chuck opens the door, I feel pretty certain this is a bachelor pad. Chuck smiles at me, but I'm pretty sure he has no idea who I am.

"I'm Magdela," I tell him, "Roberto's daughter."

"Oh, yeah," he says. "Last time I saw you, you were a little kid."

"Right." I glance away uncomfortably. Something about the black leather furniture and the animal prints is disturbing. "Uh, is my dad here?"

"No, I think maybe he went in to work today."

"On Saturday?"

"Or maybe he went apartment hunting," he says quickly. "I guess I wasn't paying attention."

"Oh."

"I'll tell him you stopped by."

"Okay." I start to leave and then turn around. "Will you ask him to call me?" I say suddenly. "Tell him it's urgent, okay?"

He nods. "Will do."

Then I go back to Claire's car. I'm sure disappointment is written all over my face, because Claire is extra sympathetic when I get in.

"Not there?"

I shake my head.

"That's too bad."

"Chuck said he was either at work or apartment hunting."

"Bummer."

"Yeah. It doesn't look like this thing is going to blow over."

"Do you think your dad will be in church tomorrow?" she asks hopefully.

I consider this. "I don't know, but I don't see why not. I mean, he's got a lot of friends there. And just because Mom's falling apart and throwing him out—well, I don't see why that would keep my dad from going. If anyone should stay away, I'd think it'd be my mom. She's the one who caused all this."

"So maybe he'll be there!" she says with enthusiasm. "Maybe you can talk to him tomorrow."

But as it turns out, he's not there. And I know this for a fact because I looked all through the sanctuary, and I never saw him anywhere. I'd even driven myself to church just to make sure I'd have my own wheels in case Dad and I went somewhere afterward. I didn't want to have to beg a ride from my mom.

"Are you showing up at Grandma's after church?" Mom asked me this morning.

"Why?"

"It's her seventy-fifth birthday, Magdela. Did you forget that Tia Louisa is making a special dinner today?"

I slapped my forehead. "Yeah, as a matter of fact, I did."

"Do you want a ride?" Mom persisted.

"No," I told her. "But I'll come. I might be a little late. But tell her I'll be there, okay?"

As it turns out, I won't be late. I even have time to stop and get her a card and a birthday balloon. But as I'm driving toward her house, I grow curious as to how my mom plans to handle Dad's absence today. Will she announce to everyone in her rather conservative and traditional Catholic Latino family that she threw my father out last weekend? Or will she keep this little bombshell to herself? I park along the street in front of my grandma's small duplex, actually enjoying the anticipation of seeing my mom taking some heat from her family. Her car is already parked in the driveway.

"Magdela!" my grandma cries as she opens the door and throws her arms around me. *"Cara mia!"*

"Abuela!" I say. "Happy birthday!"

"I'm so glad you're here. Your mama said you would be late. And you know Tia Louisa's tamales might not last that long."

"Tamales!" I say as I hand her the card and balloon. "I'm glad I got here on time."

As usual, the men are seated around the small TV in the tiny living room. But they pause, looking up from the football game as they call out greetings. I say hello, feeling faintly surprised to see there are only two—Tio Vito and Tio Eduardo. But then, my grandfather died a year ago, and of course my dad's not here. As a result, the male population of these little gatherings has dwindled considerably. Well, except for the grandkids, of which I'm the youngest. Apparently, my cousins aren't around today.

I follow my grandma back to the kitchen, where I know we'll find the women. Okay, I know it's a little archaic, but it's just how my family works—men out in the living room, women in the kitchen. To be honest, I like the familiar company of my female relatives as they prepare food. My grandma sits down at her Formica-topped table and resumes chopping tomatoes. My mom is standing by the stove helping Tia Louisa set the cornhusk-wrapped tamales over the steaming water, although Tia Louisa is calling the shots. She owns a restaurant and knows everything about cooking, so naturally she's in charge of the kitchen. Tia Dominga is at the sink washing a head of lettuce. They all say hello and welcome me, and I'm immediately given an apron and the task of peeling avocados for guacamole.

"You remember the way I showed you, Magdela?" Tia Louisa asks as she looks over my shoulder.

I nod. "Yes. And it works really well too."

She pats me on the back. "Maybe you should come work at my restaurant. I think you're doing it better than some of my prep cooks."

I laugh but don't tell her that I can't imagine anything worse than working as a prep cook, going home every night drenched in the stink of onions and grease. Major yuck!

As we work in the kitchen, no mention is made of my dad or his absence, and I am curious if my mom just made up some excuse. Perhaps she said he had to travel for his work, since he does this occasionally. This is my guess because the conversation is light and cheerful and everyone seems to be in good spirits, which would not be the case if they knew what was up. I cannot believe how tempted I am to just blow the lid off this thing. How I would love to just casually say, "Did you hear that Mom kicked my dad out of the house? And that she says the marriage is over?" But I keep my mouth shut. Not for Mom's sake, since I don't really care how she feels, but for Grandma's sake. I know this news would disturb her—a lot. Besides, it's her birthday.

But then, when the food is ready, the dining table is set, and we're all gathered around it, and after Tio Eduardo says a blessing, my other uncle makes an inquiry.

"Where did they send Roberto off to this time? Another exotic location like Des Moines?"

When my dad's job sends him traveling, it's usually to the most boring of places. We all like to tease him about this. I glance at my mom, curious as to how she's going to handle this. Being the good Christian woman that she claims to be, certainly she wouldn't tell a lie.

"To be honest," she says a bit uncomfortably, "I'm not sure where he is."

"He didn't tell you before he left?" Tia Louisa is clearly alarmed.

"Oh, he gave the number," Mom says quickly. "I just don't know for sure where the place is. It's been a busy week. Did I tell you that I may have sold the old Parker mansion?"

"Are you kidding?" says Tio Eduardo. "That's great. You'll be rich."

And just like that, the conversation switches and no one seems to be the least bit concerned about my dad anymore. I have to hand it to my mom: The woman is smooth. Even so, I can barely stand to look at her right now. If it weren't Grandma's birthday, I'd probably lose it completely and just totally spill the beans. At one point, shortly after her pathetic lie about my dad's absence, she looked directly in my eyes, almost as if she thought I was going to support her in this deception. But I just looked away.

Finally, the meal draws to an end, and I decide to excuse myself before I blow my mom's cover and spoil the fun for everyone.

"I'm sorry to eat and run," I tell them, "but I've got this big assignment that's due tomorrow and I think I'd better get home and get some homework done." Of course, this is a big fat lie. But I'm thinking what's good for Mom must be good for me, right? Maybe we'll all turn into freaking hypocrites before this thing is over.

four

I GET BACK OUT TO THE CAR AND TAKE IN A LONG DEEP BREATH AND then slowly let it out, telling myself, *Just chill before you explode.* Then I turn on my cell phone and am surprised to see I've had a call from my dad. I quickly dial his number and am even more surprised when he actually answers.

"Hi, Magpie," he says in that familiar warm voice I've been missing.

"Dad!" I practically squeal. "You finally called. I was starting to think maybe you'd left the country."

"I'm so sorry, honey. It's just that, well, it's hard to explain. But life has been pretty tough this past week. It's all I can do just to get through this."

"I know," I assure him. "And I'm so sorry."

"Yeah, me too."

"Can we meet somewhere to talk?" I ask hopefully.

"Uh, right now?"

"Well, whenever," I say with disappointment. "I just *really* want to see you, Dad. And I really need to talk."

"How about if we meet at Java Hut for coffee?" he suggests. "Will that work for you?"

"Sure," I tell him.

"In about half an hour?"

"Sounds great."

I drive straight to Java Hut. He's not there when I go inside, but that's just because I'm early. I don't really care—I'm so anxious to see him. It feels like it's been a year. I order myself a mocha and find a quiet table by the window and then take the chair that faces the door so I can watch for him. Finally, nearly thirty minutes has passed, my mocha is gone, and he's still not here. I'm about to call him to see what's up, but then I notice his dark blue Explorer just pulling up to the curb.

I rush to the door, eager to meet him. I instantly forget his lateness and my crankiness and give him a big hug. "I'm so glad to see you!" I exclaim. "I've missed you so much, Dad."

He seems almost surprised at this. But then he smiles and pats me on the cheek, and it seems like everything is just the way it used to be. We order more coffee and go sit down, and I immediately tell him about Grandma's birthday and how Mom covered for him—although I'm thinking she really covered for herself, since she could care less about him right now.

"So they don't know yet?" he asks.

I shake my head. "Nope. No one suspects a thing."

He frowns.

"Do you *want* them to know?" I ask.

Then he shrugs. "Maybe. It might be easier in the long run, Maggie."

"But why?" I ask. "Don't you think there's a chance you and Mom can work this out? Can't you get counseling at the church or something?"

He looks down at his coffee and seems truly sad. "I suppose it's worth considering."

"Claire said that Donna Fierro is a really good counselor," I say quickly. "She helped Claire's mom and stepdad work some things out a few years ago. Maybe you and Mom should make an appointment with her."

"Maybe."

And then Dad changes the subject and asks about me, like how I'm doing, how school is going. So I tell him about the SATs yesterday and my date with Brandon. And finally, we both get pretty quiet, and I'm afraid that this time is about to end.

"I'm really sorry this whole thing is happening," he tells me. "I know it's hard on you, and Elisa and Marc too. But I guess it could've been worse. Your mom and I could've split up when you kids were still little."

I want to tell him that it doesn't matter how old we are, it still hurts just the same. I'm not sure how I even know this, but I do. "You guys haven't totally given up, have you?" I ask in a meek voice.

"I think your mom has given up," he says sadly.

"But it's not just *her* choice, is it? I mean, don't you have a say here? What if you want to make things work? Doesn't she have to at least try?"

He doesn't answer.

"And what about being a Christian?" I challenge. "And all that 'until death we do part' stuff? Doesn't it matter anymore?"

"It matters, Maggie."

"So why does it have to be over, Dad? Why can't you guys work this out? Why are you just giving up so easily?"

"I'm not completely giving up."

"Meaning you'll talk to Mom about counseling?"

"I'll think about it."

I tell myself that it's better than nothing, but I do find Dad's lack of enthusiasm discouraging. Still, I try to consider how he must feel right now—how this must be really hurting him.

"I know this must be hard for you too, Dad," I say, "and I want you to understand that I'm not blaming you. I saw on a regular basis how Mom treated you, how she was always mad at you, and for nothing. I guess I can't blame you for leaving."

He doesn't say anything.

"In fact, I've suspected all along that she's the one who told you to leave." I wait for him to respond.

"It was something like that, Maggie. But she was pretty upset."

"She's always upset," I tell him. "Claire says that it could be hormones. Mom might be going through menopause."

He kind of smiles. "I don't know about that, Maggie, but I do know that she's very angry at me."

"But that's so unfair."

He shakes his head. "Not necessarily. She has reasons to be upset with me."

"Stupid reasons."

He glances at his watch now. "Sorry to cut this off, Magpie, but I need to meet someone at four . . . to look at an apartment, and it's on the other side of town."

"Need any company?" I offer, thinking this could be the perfect time to mention my interest in living with him instead of Mom.

"That's tempting," he says, smiling as he stands. "But I have some errands to run as well, so I probably should just get going."

I nod. "Well, stay in touch."

"Yeah, I'll do better," he promises. "It's just hard getting all these things figured out—everyday stuff like doing my own laundry and grocery shopping." He laughs. "Well, I guess I've been pretty spoiled by your mom."

I want to tell him that he should let me come live with him and that I could take care of all those domestic chores for him. But he's already waving good-bye and heading to the door. So I take the last swig of my second mocha as I watch him get in his Explorer and drive away. Maybe I can present that idea to him later, after he has a place of his own. I just hope he gets into an apartment that has room for two.

Naturally, I don't tell my mom about meeting with Dad. Like, what good would that do? Besides, when I get home, she seems consumed with her computer. She barely looks up to say hello, so I simply go upstairs and barricade myself in my room, pretending to do homework. Interesting that she doesn't even ask me about that. But maybe she got that I lied to the family today, just like she did, and now she's too embarrassed to ask me about it. I decide to e-mail Elisa and Marc with the latest on the parents—not that I have much to tell them. But I do mention my counseling idea and how Dad said he'd consider it. I also mention that Dad is planning to get an apartment. While that's not too encouraging, I figure they might as well know how things are looking.

I let a few days pass before I call my dad again. It's not like I want him thinking I'm this big pest. Once again, he doesn't answer. But I leave a message asking him if he found a place yet, and if I can come visit him sometime. "Maybe I could make you dinner or something," I say hopefully.

"You might have to let him go, you know," says Claire as I hang up. She's giving me a ride home from school today. In my efforts to economize, I've been leaving my car at home and bumming rides with her this week.

I instantly wish I hadn't left that message while she was listening. But I'd been waiting all day to make this call, and unfortunately, I just couldn't wait until I got home.

"What do you mean?"

"Well, if he's not calling you, maybe it's a hint, you know?"

"He's just going through a really tough time right now," I say in his defense. "He said that it's been hard just getting through the everyday stuff like doing laundry and grocery shopping, you know. I'm sure he's just busy."

"Yeah, that's probably the case." But even as she says this, I can hear the skepticism in her voice.

I remind myself that Claire's dad totally walked out on her. It's natural for her to assume that mine will do the exact same thing. But I know that my dad is different. And I realize that he's just having a hard time adjusting to "the separation." That's what my mom is officially calling it now.

"So do I get any allowance this week?" I had asked her on Monday.

She frowned. "Well, yes, of course, Maggie. But I'm a little tight right now. How about if I give you half? Your dad and I still need to work out some financial things." She pulled out some bills and sighed. "Maybe you can ask your dad for the rest."

"So that's how it is?" I asked. "I'm supposed to go begging money from Dad now? Just because you drove him away?"

Her dark eyes flashed at me. "I did *not* drive him away, Magdela. He chose to leave."

I took the money from her. "Yeah, right." I started to leave.

"You don't know everything, Miss Magdela," she said in her snippy voice. "Before you go around judging people, maybe you should get your facts straight first."

I turned around and looked at her. "What facts?"

She pressed her lips tightly together, looking as if she was trying to control herself from swearing in Spanish. "Ask your father," she seethed.

"Fine," I seethed back. "I will."

"Fine," she said as she walked away, her high heels making harsh-sounding clicks on the hardwood floor.

That's when I decided it might be time to get a job. But when I looked through the classifieds, there wasn't a whole lot going on besides retail, and I did that during the holidays last year. Talk about torture! They expect you to learn everything in a couple hours and treat rude customers like they're not, and then they let you go right after New Year's. I do not want to go through that again. So I decided that I should give my aunt a call. Okay, it was a desperate move and perhaps just a way to get my parents' attention—like, *I am so desperate I'm willing to work in Tia Louisa's restaurant*, which I've always sworn I would never do.

"I'm actually looking for a hostess," she had told me on Tuesday.

"What does a hostess do?" I asked, probably revealing my ignorance, but she is, after all, my aunt.

"She's the one up in front," Tia Louisa explained. "She takes your name and seats you at the table, you know?"

"Oh, yeah," I said eagerly since the hostess is usually nicely dressed and probably doesn't go home smelling like a deep-fried tortilla. "That would be okay."

"The hostess doesn't make much in tips," she said apologetically.

"That's okay," I assured her. "I just need some extra money now that—" Then I stopped myself.

"Now that what?" I heard the sharp tone of suspicion in her voice.

"Oh, now that I'm going to be graduating, you know, trying to save up for college."

"Oh, right."

"So when should I start?"

"How about Thursday? It won't be as busy as the weekend, and I can help train you myself."

So it was settled. I was expected to show up at Casa del Sol at four on Thursday. "To help set up tables," Tia Louisa informed me. "That's also part of your job."

"So when do you start working?" Claire asks me as she pulls up at my house.

"Tomorrow."

"You're really going through with it?"

I nod as I reach for my bag. "Yep. And my schedule will be from four to nine on Wednesdays, Thursdays, Fridays, and Saturdays."

"Man, there's the end of life as you know it."

I sigh. "So do you think my dad will feel sorry for me now?"

She laughs. "Not if he's anything like my stepdad. He'd stand up and cheer if I ever got a job."

"Yeah, but my dad wanted me to focus on school. He always said there would be plenty of time to work after college."

"Well, things have changed," Claire says in a way that makes me think she knows more about this than I do.

"But they can change back," I say as I climb out of her car.

She shrugs. "Maybe."

"Thanks for the ride." Then I walk up to the house and wonder if I'm being totally unrealistic to think that my parents will eventually figure things out and get back together. I mean, it seems entirely possible to me. And then I remind myself of the Bible verse that our youth group leader often tosses out at us: "All things are possible with God." So why not?

But as I turn my key in the door, I realize I've been leaving God pretty much out of our family's problems lately. Like, I haven't even prayed once for my parents' situation. And to be perfectly honest, I think I've been mad at God since I first heard the news. In fact, I still am. I remember that youth group is tonight and wonder if it might help my attitude to go. But I also remember that Claire won't be there because she and her mom planned to start doing some early Christmas shopping, even though it seems like we're barely past Halloween. Oh well. I'm not sure I really want to go to youth group alone. Okay, call me insecure or whatever, but I really don't like walking in there by myself. It's just the way I am. And besides, isn't it kind of hypocritical for me to go when I'm still mad at God? Shouldn't I get things straightened out first?

five

I feel unexplainably nervous as I drive to Casa del Sol for my first night on the job. I wonder if I've made a mistake, like what happens if I mess up and Tia Louisa gets mad at me? Everyone knows that my mom's older sister has a temper way worse than my mom's. What have I gotten myself into?

"Are you sure about this?" Mom asked me as I was getting ready to leave this afternoon. To my surprise, she'd come home from work early. Probably to try to talk me out of working for her sister.

"Yes," I said in a slightly defensive tone. "What? Do you think I'm incapable of being a hostess?"

"No, that's not it at all. I'm sure you'll be great, Maggie. I'm just worried about your studies. This is your senior year, you know. It's important to keep your grades high."

"I *know*, Mom. It's *my* senior year, remember? And my grades are just fine, thank you very much!"

"They are fine for now. But what about later?"

"Look, maybe I wouldn't have to get a job if you and Dad weren't making such a mess of everything. But I guess it's time for me to become more independent, to stand on my own two feet since it looks like my family is totally falling apart."

"We're not totally falling apart."

"Whatever." I glanced at my watch. "I have to go."

But now as I'm driving to work, I'm not so sure it's a good idea. Normally, I would pray about something like this, but since I've been feeling like such a hypocrite lately, I'm not so sure. Finally, I just shoot up a help-me-God kind of prayer. I hope he's listening.

"You look very nice," says Tia Louisa when I walk in five minutes early.

"Thanks." I look around the deserted restaurant. "It's not very busy."

She rolls her eyes at me. "Magdela," she says in a slightly scolding voice, "surely you know we don't open for dinner until four thirty?"

"Oh," I say, feeling stupid. "I guess I've never been here that early."

"Put your coat and purse in here," she says as she leads me to a small room with lockers off the kitchen. She hands me a padlock. "I'd like to say that I can trust all my employees, but that is not the case. You lock it up or take a chance on losing it."

So I lock my things in an empty locker and put the key in my skirt pocket. Hopefully I won't lose it. Then my aunt gives me a tour of the restaurant, which I think is kind of funny since we've been coming here for as long as I can remember and I'm pretty sure that I've seen it all before. Still, I listen and try to act like I'm really paying attention.

Then she shows me where the linens are kept and how to set the tables. Another woman—I'm guessing she's from the kitchen since she has on a white jacket—is working on the other side, setting tables too. Tia Louisa is very precise about how she wants the napkins folded and where to place the silverware.

"I'm sure you know the proper way to set a table," she says as she straightens a knife that isn't pointing directly to the water glass (the way she told me to do it), "but I want everything to look perfect." She picks up a wine goblet that has what appears to be a lipstick mark on it. "Susan," she calls, holding the goblet up. "There's a stained glass."

"Sorry, Mrs. Iago. I'll take care of it."

"You see, Magdela," Tia Louisa says in a quieter voice, "the reason for perfection is because of the image."

I nod as if I understand. "The image."

"Yes. I mean, the image that we get stuck with as Mexicans, you know? Of the old stereotypical Mexican restaurant that is not very clean or stylish or refined."

"No one can accuse you of that, Tia Louisa."

She smiles. "Yes, and that's just how I want to keep it."

I know that's her hint to me that I should be very proper and careful. And as a result, I'm feeling even more worried about making a mistake. But we quickly work our way around the tables, and I think I'm actually getting the hang of it, and by four thirty, everything really does look perfect.

My aunt pauses to adjust one of the red roses, which is hanging just slightly over the edge of the small crystal vase. "There," she says. "That should do it."

Then she explains that it's my responsibility to answer the phone and demonstrates how to take reservations. She shows me exactly where I will stand beside the wooden podium and greet the guests. She explains how I will take their names and offer to take their coats, and where I will hang them after seating a party. She makes me repeat how the numbering of the tables works and how to use the chart properly, and finally she shows me how I will escort the guests to their tables and pour their water.

"The waiters usually light the oil candles," she tells me. "If it's busy, then you can go ahead and do that. We don't want anyone sitting there in the dark. Also, when it gets busy, especially on the weekends, I'll expect you to serve beverages as well—other than wine and beer, of course. You're not old enough for that. But you can take their order and have someone from the bar handle it."

She gives me a few more tips, like to be careful to avoid the small dance floor in the corner if it's in use, and I actually wonder if I should have been taking notes the whole time. Then, just a few minutes before five, our first customers arrive: two middle-aged businessmen who explain they're from out of town and looking for an early dinner. My aunt stands on the sidelines as I offer to take their coats and then escort them to a table. So far so good. But then I'm not sure which table to put them at and finally decide on one that's off to the right. My aunt explained earlier how there are "good" tables and "better" tables and finally the "best" tables, near the big fireplace. But since the restaurant is completely empty, I choose a "better" table. I hope that's okay. I try not to slop as I pour their water, and then I tell them that their waiter will be with them shortly.

"Nicely done," she tells me. I feel as if I can take a deep breath now.

"I'll go hang up their coats," I say as I pick up the coats from where I previously stashed them (a discreet table behind the podium that my aunt explained was for this purpose).

And so it goes for the next few hours. The restaurant isn't terribly busy, just consistent. I make a few mistakes, like pouring water from a pitcher that's mostly ice and making a mess all over the table. Fortunately, Tia Louisa was in the kitchen.

Then I accidentally seated two parties in the wrong order, and the ones who had been waiting longer became a little annoyed. Of course, I apologized, but it's not like they had to wait very long—not more than five minutes, I'm sure. Still, Tia Louisa was not happy.

"It's very important to seat guests in order, Magdela—unless they have reservations, of course."

My feet are killing me by the time my shift ends at nine. I'll remember to wear more comfortable shoes next time. I go to where Tia Louisa is doing some bookwork in her office. "I guess I'm done," I say.

She removes her glasses and looks at me. "I think you're going to be fine, Magdela. Just remember that our guests always come first. It seems that whenever I fire a hostess, it's because she loses sight of that."

I nod. "I'll remember that."

"And don't forget your tips."

"Tips? I thought I didn't get any."

"Well, not much. But the waitstaff are supposed to share. Your tip jar is in the kitchen."

"Thanks."

"And make sure you let them know that you're taking it now." She kind of laughs. "That's their reminder to ante up; otherwise they might forget and take your share home with them."

So I head back to the kitchen, where everyone is looking rather limp and tired. "My aunt told me to pick up my tips."

"Over here." Manuel, the head chef, jerks his thumb toward a shelf behind him.

"Oh, wait," says Ned, one of the waiters, and not a bad-looking guy either. "I have something to add."

I feel kind of uncomfortable as I wait for him to put some money in the jar, almost as if I'm begging, but then I remind myself that this is how it works in the restaurant business.

"Thanks!" I tell him.

"Thank *you*," he says with a very cool smile. "You're a lot better than our last hostess." The others laugh and make a few unkind comments.

I grin. "Hey, that's good to hear, especially since this is my first day."

And so I'm feeling okay as I drive home. I mean, it feels kind of weird to be driving across town—by myself—at this time of night. But it also makes me feel kind of grown-up too. And I'm thinking, maybe that's what this is all about. Maybe it is time for me to grow up. That's kind of an encouraging thought, but it's also kind of depressing too. Like suddenly I'm thrust into this adult world, and I haven't even finished high school yet. It doesn't seem quite fair.

I don't count my tips until I get home, and I am surprised to see that it's nearly twenty dollars. And this wasn't even a busy night. Then I hear Mom tapping on my door. "Magdela?"

"Come in," I say in a pretty grumpy voice.

"Sorry to disturb you, but I didn't hear you come in. Everything okay?"

"Yeah."

"Look, I'm sorry I snapped at you earlier. And after you left, I got to thinking that maybe it is good for you to work. Working is a kind of education and it helps you to grow up. I just don't want you to neglect your studies."

"I don't want to neglect my studies either," I tell her in a less-than-patient tone as I toss my shoes into my cluttered closet. "I was just about to hit the books."

"Well, don't stay up too late."

"Look, Mom," I say, feeling seriously aggravated now. "I think I know when it's time to go to bed, and even when it's time to get up, for that matter. I even brush and floss my teeth without being reminded, if you haven't noticed. And if I'm going to be working in the grown-up world, maybe it's time you started treating me more like one. Just think about it: I'm going to be out on my own before long."

She nods and steps back. "Yes, you're right. Good night."

"Good night."

Okay, I do feel guilty after she leaves. I don't know why I'm being so mean to her. I've never been like that—before Mom and Dad broke up, that is. If I ever talked the least bit disrespectfully to her when Dad was around, he would always call me on it—not in a mean way, but he would remind me to respect her. And I guess it made me respect both of them. Now I don't know who to respect. I mean, I realize Dad's having a hard time and everything, but he still hasn't returned my phone call. And I'm all ready to tell him that if I can come live with him, I'll not only help out with the household chores like cooking and cleaning but I'll even contribute financially—okay, not much, but at least I can take care of my own expenses. It's got to be stretching him to pay rent and stuff for where he's staying plus covering the bills over here too. In fact, I'm wondering if Mom will have to sell the house, especially after I move out. She doesn't need this much room. Part of me doesn't care, like I want to see her suffer for what she's done, but another part of me doesn't want to give up our home either. I mean, what about holidays? And where do we go when we want to "come home"? Do parents even think about this stuff when they start breaking up marriages? It's not fair.

six

"What's up with Brandon these days?" Claire asks me as she pulls into the school parking lot. It's like the hundredth time she's brought him up this week.

"Huh?" I decide to play dumb as I absently look out the side window.

"Well, you said he's talked to you and stuff this week. So has he even hinted at asking you out again or not? And if not, why not?"

"I don't know, Claire." I try to mask my frustration as I climb out of her car. "Why don't you ask him?"

"Really?" She sounds serious as she comes around from the driver's side to join me. "You want me to?"

"Of course not!" I turn and look at her. "Are you nuts? That's like so junior high."

"Not necessarily, Maggie. I read this article in *Glamour* for women who haven't met their match yet, and the author said that women need to take control."

I laugh. "Why are you reading stupid articles like that anyway?"

"I thought I might learn something. It also said that one of the main reasons women remain single is because they are too passive when it comes to dating."

"So are you going to ask Grayson Allen out?" I ask in a teasing voice. Claire has had a crush on this guy since sixth grade.

"Yeah, right." She slugs me in the arm.

"Ouch!"

"So how was work last night? I almost forgot that it was your first day on the job. Pretty gruesome?"

"It was okay."

"Seriously?"

"Well, my aunt can be a bit of a dictator, but I kind of understand it. I mean, Casa del Sol is a pretty nice restaurant."

"Yeah. In fact, I was thinking if we go to prom this year, we should insist on having dinner there."

I laugh. "Yeah, maybe I can work my shift first and then run into the back room and change."

"Like we'll even go to prom."

"Hey, we might. And if all else fails we can resort to your women-take-control idea and just ask some guys ourselves, right?"

"Hmmm . . ." She actually seems to consider this. "But then who pays?"

"Didn't your article explain that?"

But now we're inside the school, and I don't really want to continue this discussion. I mean, how pathetic is it to overhear two senior girls making plans to invite some guys to prom when it's like six months out? We part ways, but Claire's question haunts me. Why *hasn't* Brandon asked me out again? We had a pretty good time, or at least *I* did, and he's still talking to me.

I see a poster for the Harvest Dance, which is only a week away, and I guess I hoped Brandon might want to take me to it, although that's looking less and less likely. Then I remember my new job and realize I'll probably be working that night anyway. Well, whatever.

By the end of the day, I've had one conversation with Brandon, and like our relationship, it didn't go anywhere.

"Are you going to the game tonight?" he asked me during lunch.

"No," I told him. "I have to work."

"I didn't know you had a job."

So I explain the new job and how my aunt's the owner.

"Cool," he said. "That's a great place to eat."

And that's it. End of story. I think my dating future with Brandon is a big black hole.

I tell Claire about our exchange on the way home from school and, naturally, she is sympathetic.

"Oh, Brandon's not so hot," she finally says.

"What do you mean?" I demand.

"Just that he's not like the smartest guy around, if you know what I mean."

"He's smarter than Grayson," I tease.

Then we go at it, trying to prove which guy is smarter, until we're both laughing so hard that we can't even remember what we were arguing about. Still, it feels good to laugh. It seems like it's been a long time.

"Thanks for the ride," I tell her when we reach my house. "Now that I have a job, I shouldn't be so broke."

"Hey, it's okay. I don't mind at all."

"Yeah, well, we can take turns."

"I guess I'll go to the game with Sara and Gwen tonight."

"Sounds like fun."

"Have a good night at work," she says in a voice that's a little too cheerful, like she's really feeling sorry for me and trying to make me feel better.

I force a smile. "Yeah." Even though I'm glad to have a job, I guess I still feel like I might be missing out on something—not like a date with Brandon or anything, but just going to the game with Claire and Sara and Gwen would have been fun. Kind of a girls'-night-out thing—like something I should be doing during my last year of high school instead of folding napkins and hanging up coats.

I try not to feel sorry for myself as I change my clothes for work. "You're a grown-up," I tell the mirror as I freshen my lip gloss and blush. But the Latina girl looking back at me with the big, dark, sad eyes is not convinced. I try putting my hair up, and this actually makes me look older. "Get over it," I finally tell myself as I shove my feet into a more comfortable, less fashionable pair of shoes. "Welcome to the grown-up world."

My second night on the job feels a little more natural than the first, but it is definitely busier. As soon as I walk in the door, people start calling for reservations, and not long after that, the tables are filled and the waiting list gets longer.

"If it gets really busy," Tia Louisa told me, "I'll take some of these calls in my office. Remember, your first responsibility is to make our guests feel at home."

"Right."

I do my best. I also try not to look as frantic as I feel while I take names, seat guests, pour water, hang up coats—and miss an occasional phone call, which I assume my aunt is getting. And before I know it, several hours have passed and it's nearly closing time.

"You're doing great," says Ned, my favorite waiter, as he comes up from behind me with the dessert tray balanced on one hand.

"Thanks."

My shift finally ends, and although diners still linger over coffee, dessert, and quiet music, Tia Louisa says that I can leave.

"You're doing just fine, Magdela," she tells me as I stop by her office to say good night. "I think I could make a restaurateur out of you yet."

I laugh. "Maybe so."

"It's not such a bad life," she says as she leans back in her chair. For the first time, I notice how beautiful she is—in an older-woman, gray-haired sort of way. She has this elegance and style that is really attractive.

"I'm surprised Brad and Andy don't want to work here," I tell her, referring to my cousins.

"Well, Brad's got his master's in business." She sighs. "I guess I hope that someday he'll get interested. But Andy, well . . ." She kind of laughs. "You know your cousin. He's twenty-five going on sixteen."

I don't know what to say now. I suppose I should just go, but something seems to keep me here. Maybe it's just seeing Tia Louisa at her desk looking slightly tired but still queen of her world.

"Magdela?" she says as I'm about to leave.

"Huh?"

"What's going on with your parents?"

I'm so surprised by this question that I kind of stammer around for a bit before I finally manage to say, "Why are you asking?"

She sighs and leans forward. "I know things aren't right. Last time I spoke to Rosa, she started crying. That's not like her. I asked her about Roberto, and she became even more upset. I know something is wrong with my baby sister. What is it, Magdela?"

I look at the chair on the other side of her desk.

"Sit down," she tells me. "Tell me what's going on, Magdela."

So I tell her. And I see no reason not to tell her. It's not like my parents can hide their little secret forever. When I'm finally done, I begin to cry.

Then Tia Louisa gets up from her chair, comes around to where I'm sitting, and puts her hand on my shoulder. "I'm sorry, Magdela. This must be very hard for you."

I nod without speaking, and she hands me a tissue from her desk.

"I suspected it was something like this. But do you know why?"

I wipe my nose. "Why?" I echo.

"I mean, what brought them to this place in their marriage? I know they've had their problems. Haven't we all? But your mom and dad seemed so strong in their religious convictions—all that reformed-Catholic business and their Bible study groups and such." She leans back against her desk and folds her arms across her waist. "Anyway, I figured of all the kids in our family, Rosa would be the last one to have serious marriage problems."

"Me too."

"Poor Rosa."

I study my aunt for a moment, wondering if I heard her right. "Poor Rosa?" I say. "What about my dad?"

Her brows lift. "Well, I'm sure Rosa has tried her best to hold their marriage together, Magdela. I can't imagine her giving up easily. And I know how much she loves Roberto."

"Tia Louisa," I say in a firm voice, "my mom is to blame for this. She kept nagging and picking on my dad. She was always starting fights. And I'm positive she's the one who told him to leave."

"Did you ask her about it?"

I consider this. "Yeah, well, sort of. But she never gives me any specific details. She just says it's for the best that he left—that we're better off without him—and that's just wrong."

"I'm sure there's a lot more to the story, Magdela. Only your parents know the real reasons beneath all this. Still, I know it's hard for you."

I nod.

"And it's going to be hard on everyone."

"Everyone?"

"The family. You know what we think about divorce. Mama will throw a fit."

"But just because they're separated doesn't mean they'll get divorced," I tell her. "I've talked to my dad about counseling, and he's considering it."

She nods. "Yes, well, hopefully they'll work this out."

"That's what I'm hoping." I toss the used tissue into her waste-basket and sigh. "Thanks for talking to me about it. It feels kind of good to have it out in the open—I mean with an adult." Then I feel worried. "But you're not going to tell anyone," I say quickly. "I mean in the family, especially Grandma, are you?"

"No." She shakes her head. "That's for Rosa to do. But I do plan to talk to her. I'm sure she'll understand why you told me." She kind of laughs. "I can tell her I wouldn't let you go home until I dragged it out of you. Speaking of home, you should go before it gets too late. Rosa will be worried."

As I drive home, I wonder why everyone is so quick to put the blame on Dad. Is it just the-guy-must-be-guilty prejudice? And if so, how fair is that? At the stoplight, I check my phone to see if I have any messages and am pleased to see that my dad has actually left one. Hoping the light will last, I start listening.

"Hey, Magpie, I'm moving into my apartment this weekend and just wanted to let you know. It's a real nice place with a pool and everything. Anyway, I'll be pretty busy for the next few days, but maybe after I get settled you can come over and fix me that dinner you promised. And maybe you can give me some decorating help. I have a feeling I'm going to be pretty hopeless at this. Talk to you later."

The light turns green, and I feel happier just having heard his voice. Okay, maybe not so happy that he's getting into his apartment, because that makes their separation feel even more real—more permanent. But maybe they just need space and some time to chill and eventually work some things out. And maybe if I keep bugging them they'll decide to get marriage counseling, and maybe they will get back together in time for Christmas.

So for the second time today, I pray. Forgetting my concerns about hypocrisy, I ask God to bring our family together for Christmas. After all, he did help me at work tonight, since it actually went pretty well. So maybe he'll answer this prayer too.

seven

Heavy gray clouds hang low in the sky as I drive home from church on Sunday. They look how I feel. Not exactly what you'd expect after spending the morning in church, but it's because I'm taking a serious guilt trip right now.

It figures that Father Thomas would teach on forgiveness today. Consequently, I think I'm feeling "convicted," and that doesn't feel good. In fact, it feels pretty rotten. I know without a doubt I haven't been a very good Christian these past couple of weeks, which is probably the main reason it's been hard to pray and probably a big part of the reason I've been feeling like such a hypocrite.

So all right, I get it already. I *know* that God wants me to forgive everyone. More specifically, I know that God wants me to forgive Mom, and even though it sounds impossible, I am seriously considering it. I know it won't be easy, but I don't think I have much choice—especially when I think about Father Thomas's warning. He said that God forgives us with the same measure that we forgive others. And that's scary. So I know I have to do this, and I'm thinking that the sooner I do this, the better.

As I drive up to my house, I see what looks like a U-Haul in our driveway. And then I realize that my dad's Explorer is attached to it. I park in front of the house and hop out to see what's up.

"Hey, Dad," I call out as I see him wheeling our jukebox out on a handcart. We've had that thing for years, and as far as I know, it doesn't even work. Mostly it's just been gathering dust and taking up space in the garage.

"Hey, Magpie." He smiles and then glances at his watch. "Wow, I didn't realize it was so late. You home from church already?"

"Yeah. I didn't want to stick around for coffee hour."

"But your mom did?"

"I guess." I notice what looks like the beginnings of a goatee on his chin. Also, his hair is cut different. "What's up with the new look, Dad?"

He grins kind of sheepishly as he rubs his chin. "I thought I needed a change. What do you think?"

I chuckle. "I think it's going to look good. And I like your short hair too. Very cool."

"Thanks."

"So what are you doing here?" I nod toward the trailer and jukebox.

"Just picking up some of my stuff."

"What are you going to do with that old thing?" I ask as he pauses by the trailer door.

"Oh, I thought I might mess around with it, see if I can get it to work." He wipes his palm across his damp forehead and glances over his shoulder.

"I got your message the other night. Your apartment sounds nice," I tell him as he wheels the jukebox up the ramp and onto the trailer. I peek into the dim interior to see there are already some other things in there, such as his leather chair and ottoman and some things from his office.

"Nice, but pretty sparse," he says as he positions the jukebox. "I thought I'd pick up some of my stuff while your mom is gone. I didn't want to upset her, you know."

I nod. "Need any help?"

"Sure. I just have a couple more things, and then I better scram."

So I help Dad bring out a few other things, and finally we're loading the last piece, a futon, and it's quite a struggle to fit it in. We've almost got it when we hear a car pull up—fast.

"Uh-oh," I say when I realize that it's Mom. We both look to see that she's blocked the driveway with her car and she's already out and hurrying toward us.

"What is going on?" she demands, her eyes flashing, first to Dad and then to me. "What are you two doing?"

"Just picking up some of my things." Dad gives the futon frame one last shove and then slams the door behind it.

"Your things?" Mom says as she puts her hands on her hips and glares at him. "Who says what's yours and what's mine?"

"Look, Rosa, I paid for these things—they are mine."

"Not so fast, mister. I've already done some research on this, and you have no right to come in here and start taking things."

"I have every right to take what belongs to me."

And suddenly they are both yelling and screaming at each other, and my mom is even using her Spanish swear words. Our neighbor Mrs. Flanders is actually standing on her porch watching them, and I wouldn't be surprised if she calls 911.

"Stop it!" I yell, moving to stand between them. "Stop it!"

And it seems I've gotten their attention, because they stop.

"You guys are acting like children, fighting over your toys. It's just stuff, you know!"

"So you think it's okay for your dad to come in here and take everything while I'm gone?" my mom demands. Her face is flushed and I can tell she's close to tears.

"He needs some things for his place."

"Let him buy his own things," Mom shoots back at me.

"But these *are* his things," I say.

"No, Magdela." She's seething now. "These are *our* things. And they should stay in *our* house until a court decides who gets what. Your dad chose to leave this marriage, and as a result, he'll have to leave all this behind."

"But that's not fair," I attempt.

"All's fair in love and war—and this is war!"

"Why are you acting like this?" I demand. "Why have you turned into such a witch? It's no wonder Dad is leaving you. I want to leave you too!"

My mom looks like she's about to explode, but she presses her lips together and glares at me as if I'm the one to blame for all this. "Fine!" she yells. "Let him take everything. Let him ruin my house, just like he's ruined my life!" And then she storms off to her car and tears off down the street, tires screeching.

I am shaking all over now, and tears are pouring down my cheeks.

"I'm so sorry, Magpie." My dad puts his arms around me and pulls me into a tight hug. "You shouldn't be caught in the middle of this. I'm so sorry."

And I just cry into his jacket and wish I were five years old again. I wish that my brother and sister were still living at home and that Mom was in the kitchen, humming to her Latino music as she makes us some lunch, and that we'd all sit down together around the big island in the kitchen and eat and talk and laugh—just the way we used to do.

"I'm sorry too, Dad," I finally say. I step back and wipe my wet face on the sleeve of my sweater. "I don't know why Mom is like this."

"She's hurting too, Maggie," he says sadly. "We all are."

"But she's being so unreasonable, so out of control. I don't see why she has to act like this."

"Situations like this bring out the worst in everyone, Maggie."

I look at him. "Not you."

"Don't be so sure."

"Well, I think you have every right to take what you need from the house," I tell him. "And if you need any more help, let me know."

He shakes his head. "No, that's fine. And I probably should go before your mom comes back with enforcements." He winks at me.

"Yeah, I can just imagine her hauling Tio Eduardo and Tio Vito back here to beat you up."

"Hey, don't joke about it. Stuff like that used to happen in situations like this, back when we were kids. Families didn't take this kind of thing lightly."

"I know, Dad. I don't think they take it lightly nowadays either."

"Thanks for the help," he says as he gets into his car, "and for the moral support. I'll give you a call later this week, once I've gotten more settled, and you can come over and check out the new digs."

I nod. "Thanks."

Then I stand in the driveway and watch as he pulls out and drives down the street. I wish I were going with him. I turn and look at our house. No way do I want to go in there now. And no way do I want to be home when my mom gets back. Who knows what that woman might do? Probably go ballistic at me for aiding my dad. So I get back into my car and just drive around. I consider calling Claire, but I don't really like to bug her family on a Sunday, especially since I saw her sitting with her family at church today. That doesn't happen too often with them since her parents sometimes work on the weekends. I don't want to interrupt a "family day."

So I go to the mall. I know it's pathetic, but it's starting to rain and I can't think of anyplace else that's not cold and wet. And I just walk around. Naturally, there are Christmas decorations everywhere, and it's not even Thanksgiving yet.

I try not to look at families, but it's like that's all I see. And I know that's ridiculous, because I'm sure there are lots of people here who aren't with their families, but it seems like each time I look up, I see another happy family. A dad with his arm around the mom and a couple of kids trailing along. A lot of them look like they've just been at church. Even when I go to the food court, I see them. Finally, I can't take it anymore and I have to leave.

I consider going to my grandma's, and I'm sure she'd enjoy the visit. I know she's been lonely since my grandpa died. But I also know that if I stopped in, I'd probably spill the beans, and then my mom would really be furious at me. So I just drive around a while. Finally, I give up my resolve. It's nearly three, and I figure Claire's probably had enough family time by now, so I call her.

"What's up?" she asks.

Just the sound of her voice makes me start to cry. I try to explain, but I'm just blubbering.

"Want me to come over and pick you up?" she offers with real concern in her voice.

I manage to convey that I'm in my car. "Just a few blocks from your house."

"Well, get on over here," she commands me. "Are you like nuts?"

It's pouring by the time I get to her house, and I get fairly wet just running up to the door, but Claire opens it quickly and gives me a hug. Then we go up to her room and I pour out the whole story.

"Yeah," she says when I'm finally done. "I can remember stuff like that. My parents fought over everything. It was horrible. It got even worse when they went through the divorce. And then there was the crud with alimony and child support." She just shakes her head. "Makes you want to be really careful if you ever get married."

"I don't think I'll ever get married," I tell her.

"You say that now, but you'll probably feel different when Mr. Right comes along."

We hang together for the rest of the afternoon. We consider going out and doing something, but it's so cold and nasty out that we decide to just watch movies from the eighties and nineties as we pig out on a pan of brownies that we baked just long enough to get good and gooey. We sit in the family room and use spoons to eat the brown glop straight from the pan.

"You know," I say to Claire, "chocolate and old Meg Ryan movies are a pretty good distraction right now."

"Better watch out though," she teases. "You could end up looking like Aunt Betty." That's Claire's aunt, who is so obese that she can't leave her house without assistance.

I drop the spoon in the pan. "Thanks for that lovely image," I tell her.

She laughs as she dips her spoon in again. "All right, my strategy worked. I get the rest of this to myself!"

Finally, I know that it's time for me to go home. I've already managed to get myself invited for dinner, and now it's getting late.

I have my cell phone turned off, just in case Mom is trying to reach me. And I happen to know that Claire's stepdad has been online all afternoon, which ties up their phone line. So, short of Mom showing up here, I've been safe. Still, I know that I better go.

"Thanks for the haven," I tell Claire as I head for the door.

"Anytime," she says. "Oh, yeah, I didn't want to tell you this—I mean, while you were so bummed about your parents and everything."

"What?" I say, knowing that she's probably keeping something terrible from me.

"Well, I was at youth group last night, you know, and Kyle and I were just talking and joking around, you know, and you'll never guess what happened."

"He proposed and you guys eloped and now twins are on the way?"

She laughs and punches me in the arm. "At least you still have your sense of humor."

"Yeah, right. But tell me . . . what happened?"

"We decided to go to the Harvest Dance together."

"Oh."

"See, I knew it would just make you feel bad."

"No," I say quickly, "you know I have to work that night anyway—as if it matters. Really, I'm glad for you. And Kyle's a nice guy." Then I narrow my eyes at her. "But tell me the honest truth: Did you follow the advice in that magazine article and ask him first?"

She grins mischievously. "Well, let's just say I did some heavy hinting."

I pat her on the back. "Well, good for you. And, really, I'm glad for you. I really am."

"Thanks."

It's still rainy and cold when I go outside, but I do feel a little better now than when I got here—well, other than finding out that Claire is going to the Harvest Dance. Before, it seemed like she was the only one besides me who wasn't going. Selfish as it is, it made me feel better. Oh well.

When I get home, the house is dark. Mom's car isn't in the driveway, but I know it could be in the garage, especially now that there's more room.

I unlock the door and tiptoe inside. I'm hoping to get to my room without having to talk to my mom. I have no idea how she's going to treat me after I showed my allegiance to Dad today. Like she said, *this is war.* And I have a feeling that she now considers me the enemy too.

I do a pretty pathetic job on my homework, but I'm in a hurry to be done and relieved that so far my mom hasn't barged in here and started yelling at me. I blame the poor quality of my English paper on my home life and even imagine myself sitting in the academic counselor's office and telling Mr. Hurley that it's all my parents' fault that I'm failing my senior year.

Then I put my books and stuff away and quietly get ready for bed. It's not even ten thirty, but I figure my chances of avoiding the mom-confrontation will improve if it looks like I'm asleep. Then I turn off my light and hop into bed. Of course, I don't feel the least bit sleepy, and I miss the music that I usually listen to as I drift to sleep. But I don't want to chance getting up and putting it on and having Mom bust in here to read me the riot act.

And so I lie in my bed and just think. I remember how I had a hard time going to sleep when I was little and how my mom told me to pray myself to sleep. She taught me how to do the "A to Z

Prayer," and I would say, "Thank you, God, for apples. Thank you, God, for bubblegum. Thank you, God, for Christmas." And usually by the time I reached G, I would be asleep. I consider trying this again tonight, but then I remember Father Thomas's words.

"A state of unforgiveness will hinder your prayer life. How can you ask God for something when you know that you are living in direct disobedience to his will? Forgive first. Then come to God with your requests."

Forgive? Yeah right. Like I can forgive my mom for that horrible scene she pulled in the driveway today. Forgive her for treating my dad like dirt? Forgive her for throwing him out? How does a person forgive those kinds of things? I saw the pain in Dad's eyes when she lashed into him. I know how badly he's hurting. How can I forgive her for this?

eight

TALK ABOUT SHIPS IN THE NIGHT. IT'S LIKE MOM AND I DON'T EVEN LIVE in the same house anymore. I literally have not seen her since the big blowout on Sunday, and now it's Tuesday. I'm starting to think this might be the only way to survive this thing—Mom and I just living our separate lives until I graduate and get out of here. I'm highly motivated to ask Dad about being his new roommate.

And I'm feeling hopeful because I check my messages on our way home from school to discover he's called. He's inviting me to come check out his new digs today. "And I'll take you up on that offer to make dinner," he says, "if it's still good." So I call him back, and he gives me directions and says to meet him there at five thirty.

"What are you fixing?" Claire asks after I hang up.

"Spaghetti," I tell her. "It's about the only thing I know how to make. And that's only because we use Ragu."

"Well, that's better than *my* specialty."

"You mean frozen dinners?" I tease as she pulls in front of my house.

"Hey, they're supposed to be nutritious." She glances at the driveway. "Looks like your mom's home."

I turn and am surprised to see her car. "Yeah," I say as I gather my stuff, "I wonder what's up."

"You guys still not speaking?"

"Sort of. Mostly we don't even see each other."

"That's so weird. I mean, there are times when I wish I could go for days without seeing my parents, but it'd probably bug me too."

"Well, this is probably for the best—for now anyway."

Then I thank Claire for the ride and brace myself before going into the house. This is pretty early for Mom to be home, and I have no idea what to expect. I walk into the house but don't see or hear her. I pause in the foyer for a moment, trying to decide whether to head to the kitchen like I usually do or just duck up to my room and avoid any possible confrontations. As I'm standing there, I can't help but notice how our house looks kind of weird. There are still these holes or gaps where furniture and things are missing—the things my dad took with him to the apartment. I mean, it's not like we're hurting. We still have plenty of stuff, but it's obvious that some things have been removed. And I'm kind of surprised my mom didn't do some rearranging, especially since she usually really cares about how things look. I mean, if you move a chair or table out of place, she will notice and put it back where it had been. It's just how she is—or rather, how she was. Now I don't even know *who* she is. I'm not sure that I even want to know or that I care.

Confident that she's not downstairs, I grab a soda from the fridge and then go up to my room. I figure I can just chill for a while, and if I get lucky, she'll take off to go show a house or something. That's usually what she's doing this time of day. I doze off while reading *Twelfth Night*—go figure—and when I wake up, it's almost five and I remember that I'm supposed to meet my dad.

But when I go downstairs to scavenge some groceries for dinner, I am surprised—make that *shocked*—to see that Mom is cooking.

"Magdela," she says, looking up from where she is browning some hamburger. "How are you?"

I kind of blink. "Uh, I'm fine. What are you doing?" Okay, I realize it's a stupid question, but I'm kind of stuck.

"Cooking dinner," she says.

"For who?"

She looks at me funny. "For us."

"But I'm not going to be home tonight."

I can't tell whether she's disappointed or angry. "But I thought you only worked Wednesday through Saturday nights."

"That's not it. I mean, I don't work tonight, but I've already made plans."

"Can you change them? I thought maybe we could talk tonight, honey."

"No," I say quickly, "I can't change them. I mean, I'll be working the rest of the week and this is the only night—"

"What are you doing tonight?"

I feel defensive and want to tell her it's none of her business. But then, I suppose, that's not really true. "I'm going to Dad's," I say in a tone that I hope sounds nonnegotiable.

Her eyebrows arch, but she doesn't say anything.

"Sorry," I say. "I would've told you if I'd known you were fixing dinner and everything."

She still says nothing, turning her attention to stirring the sizzling meat.

"I want to see his new place," I explain to the back of her head. "I told him I'd fix dinner."

She turns around and looks at me, but I can't read her expression. It's almost like she's curious. "Really?"

"Yeah."

"Just you and him?"

"Yeah."

"Oh."

Now I'm thinking, *Okay, maybe she's fine with this.* "Do you mind if I take some spaghetti and stuff?"

She just shrugs and turns down the burner, putting a lid on the meat. "Do what you like, Magdela."

Then she walks out of the kitchen, and I'm still not sure whether she's angry or hurt. Why does she have to be like this? I get a bag from beneath the sink and quickly fill it with the things I think I'll need: pasta and Ragu from the pantry and then a few things from the fridge for a salad. I am just putting some Parmesan cheese in my bag when Mom comes back into the kitchen.

"Don't take that," she says, eyeing the green container in my hand.

"Huh?"

"The Parmesan cheese," she says in an aggravated tone.

"Why?"

"Because." Her voice is just a little louder now and a bit higher.

"But it's for the spaghetti," I say.

"Leave it here," she commands me.

"But it—"

"Leave the cheese *here!*" she shouts.

I open the fridge, shove the container onto the shelf, and then slam the door so hard it rattles.

"Magdela!"

"What, *Mom*?" I'm glaring at her now. I don't know why she has to act like this, like she's four years old and determined to throw a temper tantrum if she doesn't get her Parmesan cheese, for Pete's sake!

"Nothing!" Then she turns and walks out.

Okay, I'm tempted to get the cheese now, but I decide that's immature. Why sink to her childish level? But as I start my car, I can't help but think my mom is losing it. She is seriously losing it! I stop at a store and buy some Parmesan, even though I'm a little surprised at how much it costs. I figured it would be a couple of bucks. Still, it was probably Dad's money that paid for it in the first place. Mom doesn't have to be so selfish!

I try to chill as I drive across town. So my mom's disturbed. What's new? I follow my dad's directions until I come to what looks like a recently built section of town houses. Even the landscaping looks pretty new, and nicely done too. I park in the guest area that he told me about and go up the stairs marked units 35 and 36. I knock on the door with number 35 on it.

"It's open," he calls from within, and I open the door and go inside.

"Hey, this is nice, Dad," I say as I look around the open living area.

"Check out that view," he says.

I set my grocery bag on the black granite island and go across the room to look out the glass doors, which lead to a terrace that overlooks a small man-made lake rimmed with trees and walking trails. "Not bad," I tell him.

Then he gives me a brief tour, starting with the master bedroom. A large bed is all set up, complete with some plush-looking bedding in trendy tones of black and tan and silver—nothing like my mom would ever pick out, since she likes flowers and pastels. "You got a bed," I say.

"That futon wasn't going to cut it," he tells me. "Do you like it?"

"Yeah, very cool."

"After sleeping on Chuck's couch for a couple of weeks, I figured it would be cheaper to buy a good bed than see the chiropractor every week."

I smile. "Yeah, I guess so."

Then he shows me the second bedroom, which is pretty sparse, other than the futon and his desk.

"Two bedrooms," I say with interest.

"Yeah, I'm using this as my home office for now."

"Here's the other bath," he says as he opens another door.

"Nice," I tell him as I look at the spacious bathroom. "But what's up with these sinister-looking black towels? I noticed you had them in the master bath too."

"I thought it might be a safe choice for a guy who's never done laundry before. But the saleslady told me to prewash them, so I threw them in with some other things. The towels came out just fine, but all my white socks and underwear are this depressing shade of prison gray now."

I laugh. "Okay, Dad, the first rule of laundry is to wash lights with lights and darks with darks. Got that?"

He nods. "I do now."

"Well, I like your place," I say as we go back to the living room. "I mean, it looks like a guy place, but it has potential."

"I need to get a few more things," he says as I go into the kitchen and start unloading my bag.

"I assume you have pots and pans and stuff," I say, looking around the very tidy-looking kitchen.

He proudly shows me some of his recent purchases. "These pans are supposed to be foolproof," he says and hands me a heavy saucepan. "Is this big enough for the pasta?"

"I guess it'll have to be."

I start puttering around the kitchen, and to my relief, Dad goes and busies himself doing something else. I'm not ready to have him watch me cook. Soon I hear music.

"Is that the jukebox?" I ask as I pour some salt into the pan of water.

"No, it's just a CD."

"What is it?" I call.

"Jazz. John Coltrane."

"Oh." I think about this as I rinse the lettuce in the sink. I didn't even know that my dad liked jazz.

Before long, something that resembles dinner is ready. Dad has set the island with dishes I have never seen before. A very modern design, or maybe Asian, but they are squarish and about the same color as a tomato. He's also lit a candle, and I'm thinking how this all seems so very un-Dad-like. I've never seen him take any interest in things like dishes and candles and towels, and I guess I'm wondering what's up. We sit on metal barstools on either side of the island and begin to eat. I can't help but notice he doesn't ask a blessing like he used to when he was at home. But I don't mention it. It's just one more thing that's changed. But why?

We're just about done eating dinner when curiosity gets the best of me. "Okay, Dad," I say, setting down my fork, "what's with all this?"

He looks surprised. "What?"

71

"Fancy dishes, cool pans, black towels, very modern bedding. It's just so weird—so unlike you."

"Unlike me?" He frowns. "How do you know that?"

I shrug. "Well, it's unlike anything you and Mom picked out for our house."

"Your mom picked out most of the things for our house, Maggie. Well, other than my leather chair, which I insisted on purchasing, and some of the other things I picked up the other day when—" He looks at his plate.

"When Mom threw her hissy fit?"

He nods.

"So you're saying you don't like the things at our house?" I persist. "That your taste is different than Mom's?"

"Oh, I don't know, Magpie." He stands and begins clearing the dishes, setting them carefully in the sink. "I guess I don't really know who I am or what I like anymore. But maybe it's about time I started to figure it out."

"Kind of like the goatee and haircut?"

He nods as he rinses a plate. "Yeah."

"The goatee is filling in pretty good," I say.

He smiles. "Yeah, I kind of like it."

"How come you didn't grow one before?"

"Your mom." He puts a plate in the stainless steel dishwasher. "She hates any kind of facial hair."

"Oh." I reach for the sponge and start wiping down the black granite. I can almost see my reflection on the shiny surface.

"I got some ice cream for dessert," he says as he puts the last fork into the dishwasher. "Rocky Road."

"All right!" I say as I go to the cupboard for bowls. They too are square and modern-looking, but they're starting to grow on me, and I'm beginning to think they are very stylish and chic.

"I never knew my dad was such a cool guy," I say as we sit back down at the counter.

He laughs. "Well, people change, Magpie."

I hold my spoon up as if I'm toasting him. "Here's to change, Dad."

He holds his up too. "To change."

nine

I FEEL SOMEWHAT RELIEVED TO GO TO WORK ON WEDNESDAY AND Thursday, but when Friday comes around and I hear some of my friends at school—specifically Claire, Sara, and Gwen—talking about the Harvest Dance and what they're wearing and how they're doing their hair, well, it's just not that easy to go to work.

As I drive to the restaurant, I tell myself to get over it. But just as I'm parking in back, I realize Casa del Sol is exactly the kind of place where kids go to eat dinner before a dance like this, and I realize it's entirely possible I could actually be seating friends and acquaintances from school tonight. And for some reason, I find this totally mortifying.

As I put my coat and purse into my locker, I find myself feeling more and more freaked over this possibility. *Why didn't I call in sick?* I lean my head against the locker and groan.

"You okay?"

I stand up straight to see Ned staring at me, probably wondering if he needs to administer CPR or call for help.

"Yeah," I say in a glum voice, "I'm just peachy."

"What's wrong?"

And because he seems sincerely interested and because he has the nicest blue eyes, I tell him all about my panic attack over this stupid Harvest Dance crud. "Pretty juvenile, huh?" I finally say.

"Why aren't you going to the Harvest Dance yourself?" he asks. "I'm sure your aunt could've covered for you."

Now I'm embarrassed, but I decide to take it head-on. "I wasn't asked to the dance."

He looks truly surprised. "I can't believe a girl as pretty and nice as you wasn't asked to the dance. What's wrong with guys nowadays?"

I have to laugh. "I don't know," I tell him. "I think they should all get their heads examined."

"Most definitely."

And so working tonight is not nearly as bad as I'd imagined. And every once in a while, like when I was seating Ashley Gordon and Ty Banner at the "best" table next to the fireplace, Ned gave me this sweet little smile and a knowing wink, and I instantly felt better.

Because we're so busy the time flies, and before I know it my shift comes to an end. But when I go to say good night to my aunt, I find her brother—Tio Eduardo—in her office instead. He is a part owner in the restaurant, but so far I've hardly ever seen him around here.

"Where's Tia Louisa?" I ask.

"Didn't you hear? She got one of her migraines earlier tonight."

"No, it was so busy. I must've missed that. I hope she's okay."

He frowns. "She just got a new prescription. Hopefully it'll work."

"Yes, I hope so. Well, good night, then."

"Wait, Magdela," he says, pointing to the chair by the desk. "Have a seat."

Okay, now I'm bracing myself. I'm sure he's heard the news about my parents, and being that he's Mom's older brother, he's probably ready to take up her side and go pound some sense into my dad.

"I heard you missed some big dance at your school tonight?"

I'm surprised he would know about this. Maybe my mom told him—not that she's been paying attention to my life lately. "Well, sort of," I admit. "The Harvest Dance. But it's not like I was planning to go. How did you know anyway?"

"Ned told me."

"Ned?" Now I feel mixed emotions. On one hand, I'm relieved my uncle's not keeping me here to find out about my parents' marital problems, but on the other hand, I don't know why Ned had to go and tell Tio Eduardo about the dance.

He holds up his hands. "Now, don't go getting mad, Magdela."

"I'm not mad." Of course, I'm sure my face says something different.

"I just thought we should have a little chat. You're my youngest niece, and sometimes I don't think I know you very well. Louisa is very impressed with your work here."

"Really?" I feel myself perking up now. Louisa is hard to impress, and for her to mention this to someone in the family, well, that's pretty nice.

"Yes. She thinks you have real potential."

"Well, I like working here. It's a lot—"

"Ready?"

I turn to see Ned standing in the doorway now. "Huh?"

"May I take her?"

Tio Eduardo folds his hands together on the desk in a knowing and self-satisfied way and then nods and smiles, almost as if he's hatched some sort of plan. Then Ned reaches for my hand. "Right this way, miss." And he leads me back into the restaurant, where only a few tables are filled—with the "lingerers," as we call them. But Ned leads me over to the "best" table by the fire. And it's been reset and the candle is lit, and the next thing I know, Susan brings us each a plate (which turns out to be leftovers, but who's complaining?), and we sit there and enjoy a very nice meal together. I find out that he's twenty and putting himself through college—just community college for now, but he plans to transfer next fall.

"I should've worked harder to get a scholarship when I was in high school," he says. "The counselor kept telling me it was possible."

"So why didn't you?"

He shrugs. "I was too into having a good time, I guess—kind of into partying, if you know what I mean."

I nod. "Yeah. I've sort of tried to avoid that scene."

"Smart girl."

"So you're not into partying anymore?"

He laughs. "Not now that I have to support myself and pay my own tuition. No time for that stuff."

"Maybe that's for the best."

"Yeah, maybe. But I'll admit, I still miss it sometimes. I guess that's why I wanted you to have some fun tonight—I mean, since this is your senior year and everything. You know what they say about all work and no play."

"Yes!" I say with enthusiasm. "I was feeling just like that today, like everyone was out there having fun except for me. *Pity party for one, please.*"

He laughs and we talk some more. And I guess I'm thinking that maybe I was really lucky Brandon didn't ask me to the dance tonight, because I probably would've asked for the night off, and Tia Louisa probably would've given it to me, and then I would've missed all this.

A dessert of flan garnished with berries and whipped cream is served by none other than Tio Eduardo. He bows elegantly and then slyly winks at me before he exits to the kitchen.

"Care to dance?" asks Ned after we finish our desserts.

I do, so we go over to the tiny dance area and actually dance for a couple of songs.

All in all, it's very fun and a little bit romantic. Oh, I suspect that Ned is just feeling sorry for me and trying to be nice, but I can tell he and the others went to a bit of trouble to set this up.

"Thanks," I tell him when it's finally time for the evening to end. "Now I will always remember the night of the Harvest Dance during my senior year." I grin at him.

"Good. And I guess I can be grateful to the Neanderthals who didn't have the good sense to ask you out."

Ned walks me to my car, and I almost think he's going to kiss me, but instead he just makes this little bow and says, "Good night."

I feel like I'm floating as I drive home. Ned is such a nice guy. I wonder if it's possible that he really could like me. Then I almost run a red light, and I realize I better concentrate on my driving instead of daydreaming about Ned Schlamowski.

When I get home, I'm still feeling a slight rush. Back in the old days, before Mom started acting so mean, I probably would've gone and told her all about it—but not tonight. Tonight I take it to bed with me, just like I used to do when I was little and liked to sneak cookies up to my room.

But I do e-mail Claire. I ask about her evening and tell her all the details of mine, probably making it sound even better than it was, if that's possible. Then I notice that I have an e-mail from Elisa, wanting an update on the parental situation. So I fill her in as best I can, telling her about Dad's apartment and how Mom threw a fit over the Parmesan cheese. Then I decide to copy Marc on it to save writing the whole thing again. I tell them that I don't know what to do and that it doesn't look as if they'll be going in for marriage counseling anytime soon, and certainly not in time for Thanksgiving, which is next week. I know that Elisa has other plans, but I'm not sure about Marc. And I guess that's not really my problem, but it does make me sad. I have a feeling that all of our extended family will know everything by Thanksgiving. I'll leave that mess for my parents to clean up. A girl can only do so much.

Then I get ready for bed. Before I turn off the light, I stand and study myself in the mirror. I try to imagine how Ned sees me: just a pathetic Latina high school girl who couldn't even score a date for a dance, or his boss's niece who he wants to be nice to in order to maintain job security? Or perhaps he sees an interesting young woman he'd like to get to know better. I've never gone out with a guy so much older than me. But then again, I'll be eighteen in a few months, and that doesn't sound too young for twenty. I pile my hair up, squaring my shoulders and standing straighter—my sophisticated look—and I imagine what it would feel like to be Mrs. Schlamowski—well, if I believed in marriage, that is. I'm not entirely sure that I do. I let my hair drop back down, hanging in loose curls around my shoulders, and then jump into bed.

The weekend passes somewhat uneventfully. It turns out that Ned isn't even working Saturday night, and I feel a real wave of disappointment. I'd gotten dressed up especially nice and put my hair up—going for that older look—just to impress him. But at least I get paid. Tia Louisa hands me my first check, and I feel like I've won the lottery.

"Cool," I say. "I wish there was a bank open so I could cash it."

She smiles. "I suppose I could cash it for you, Magdela, if you don't tell any of the other employees."

So I take her up on the offer and feel very excited to have so much cash in my purse as I drive home. Okay, it probably wouldn't seem like much to most people, but it's a big deal to me. I mean, I actually earned this money myself, and besides occasional baby-sitting, which I don't even do anymore, this is the first time I've worked for my own money. It's pretty cool. As I drive, I try to decide what I'll do with it: save it or spend it. Probably a little of both.

I go to church Sunday morning even though I really don't want to go. But I'd rather go than have to explain to Mom why I'm skipping out on it. At least I don't have to ride with her. She seems to get that now, and she doesn't even ask anymore.

I'm glad Father Thomas has moved on from forgiveness this week. His sermon today is about being thankful, which I'm sure is because of Thanksgiving. But as I'm sitting here by myself in the back of the church, I do not feel the slightest bit thankful. For what? A crazy mom? A dad who's reinventing himself? Siblings who live far away and probably don't really care about what I'm going through as long as everyone gets it together by Christmas? Seriously, why should I feel thankful?

Then I remind myself that I *do* have some friends, like Claire, for instance, who I really should be thankful for. And then there's Ned and the possibility of romance. I consider that for quite a while.

I'm sure daydreaming in church is probably a sin, but I really can't help myself. Besides, it cheers me up a little—is there anything wrong with that? When the service ends, I'm surprised to feel slightly hopeful. Was it a result of church or my daydreaming? Who knows? But as we bow our heads for the final blessing, I think that maybe something is going to change this week. Maybe Mom will realize what a witch she's been and Dad will come to his senses and we'll all happily eat turkey together at Tia Louisa's big house on the hill. It could happen! And yes, pigs could probably fly too.

ten

"What are you doing today?" Claire asks me after church.

I shrug. "I don't know."

"Mom and Adam want to drive up to Lamberg for lunch." She glances over her shoulder and then makes a face. "It's that little inn where they had their honeymoon, you know, and I will do anything to get out of it. Can't you invite me to do something?"

I consider this. "Wanna go to the mall?" I hold up my purse like a trophy. "I got paid last night."

Claire grabs my arm. "Perfect. Let me go tell them. Oh, is your car here?"

I nod, and within minutes we're set. I even inform my mom of our plans, and she actually seems to appreciate this. She smiles and says, "Have fun."

And so we do. Claire the shopping queen is thrilled that I actually have money to spend. She puts forth her best effort to ensure I spend most of it. But I end up getting some very cool things, and some of them are pretty good deals too. I don't know if Claire notices or not, but I try to pick out things that seem more mature and sophisticated than usual. I really want to start dressing like I'm older. As we shop, she fills me in on the details of the dance, and I tell her a little more about Ned.

"He sounds hot!" she says when we finally take a coffee break in the afternoon. "Do you think it could get serious?"

"I don't know." I blow on my mocha.

"What would your parents think?"

I roll my eyes. "What do you think they'd think?"

"Well, they've been kind of distracted lately. Maybe they wouldn't notice."

"Yeah," I say hopefully. "Assuming anything will actually happen between Ned and me. He could've just been being nice." I make a dramatic, romantic sigh for Claire's benefit. "But it was *very* nice."

She laughs. "I'll have to stop in at the restaurant and get a look at this guy sometime."

"Yeah, do! Just don't let him know that's why you're there."

It's almost six when I finally get home. I park in the driveway and lug in my bags, surprised at how much I got today. I can't wait to go to my room and check them out. Maybe I'll try everything on again and really work on this new, older, more sophisticated look I'm going for.

"What is that?" my mom asks when she sees me heading for the stairs.

"Huh?"

"All those bags." She gets up from the couch where she had been reading the paper and walks over.

I hold up the bags. "Just some things I got at the mall."

She frowns. "But how? Where did you get the money?"

I exhale loudly. "I have a job, Mom. Or haven't you noticed?"

"So you got paid?"

"Yeah. On Saturday."

"How did you cash the check?"

Now I'm feeling really exasperated, like why is this her business anyway? "Tia Louisa cashed it for me."

Mom just shakes her head. "So you blew your whole check on clothes?"

I just look at her now.

"You wasted all your money, Magdela?"

"I spent it, Mom. It was *my* money and I spent it. And I didn't spend it all."

"How much do you have left?"

"Why is that your business?" I demand now. "What? Do you need a loan or something?" Okay, I stepped over the line, but I'm just so aggravated by her gestapo line of questioning. Her eyes are flashing and I'm not backing down. We get into one of the worst fights ever. If I weren't so mad, I'm sure I'd be in tears by now.

"I can't believe you!" I shout at her. "You've driven Dad away, and you are driving me away too. No one is going to want to be around you, Mom. You're going to end up a lonely, bitter, old woman with no one who even cares whether you live or die!"

"I did *not* drive your dad away. He left because he wanted to leave."

"Well, I don't blame him for leaving. I want to leave too. Dad would be so much better to live with than you. I don't see why kids don't get a choice in this stuff. If I could, I would live with him instead of you—any day!"

"Fine!" she yells. "Go and live with your precious dad. See how that works for you, Magdela. See if I care!" Then she rushes past me and up the stairs, slamming her bedroom door so loudly that I think it might fall off its hinges. And I'm so enraged that I turn around and walk out the front door with my bags and start driving across town to Dad's place to tell him that Mom is losing her mind and that I cannot stand to stay with her anymore. I know he'll understand.

I consider calling him on the way over, but it's bad enough driving under the influence of anger that I decide not to risk a phone call too. At the town house, the porch light is on, and I can see through the blurry glass door that there's light inside too. It's a dim light, but I suspect he's home. I knock on the door, and when he doesn't answer, I try the knob to find it's unlocked, so I open the door. I hear jazz music playing and figure that means he's home.

"Hey, Dad?" I call as I go into the living area. The black granite island is nicely set for dinner, similar to when I was here last week, only there's also an open bottle of red wine and a tall slender vase with one exotic-looking flower in it, maybe some kind of orchid. But what really gets my attention is that there are two place settings. Dad obviously has company.

"Magdela!" he says in a voice that doesn't sound quite right.

I turn around to see my dad and a woman I don't recognize coming down the hallway.

"What are you doing here?" he asks as he gets closer.

I'm sure my eyes are huge, and I can feel my heart pounding in my throat. It's crystal clear what's going on in here. Without even speaking, I turn and make a run for it. I throw open the door and sprint down the stairs. I can hear Dad calling my name, telling me to come back, that we need to talk. But I have no intention of talking to him. Not now. Maybe not ever.

I drive away, not even sure where I'm going. When I finally stop, it's at some stoplights, somewhere downtown I think. I look up at the red light to see that it's blurry and fuzzy and misshapen, and I realize I'm crying. I don't know what to do. I just sit there at the stoplight as it turns green then yellow then red again, and I cry.

Finally, I hear a horn honking. The light is green again, so I begin to drive. I don't know where to go, and I feel like a homeless orphan.

I know I can probably call Claire and beg to spend the night, but it's Sunday and her mom has a strict no-sleepover rule for school nights. I think my situation could be an exception, but still, I'm not sure. I consider going to Grandma's, but then I'd have to tell her about my parents, and that might give her a stroke. She already takes blood pressure medicine. Finally, I think about Tia Louisa. At least she knows what's going on, so I decide to call. I briefly fill her in on the situation, and she assures me I'm completely welcome to stay with her. "But only until this gets straightened out," she assures me in her no-nonsense voice. "And we will have to call your mother and let her know you're here."

I agree to this and slowly drive over to where she lives on the hill. It's a nice neighborhood with large older homes. I remember how my aunt and uncle made jokes when they moved there, saying how the neighbors would probably throw fits when they found out "the Mexicans" had moved in. But that was more than ten years ago, and I think they were eventually accepted. "It helps that we didn't paint the house fuchsia," my uncle likes to tease, "and we haven't put out any south-of-the-border lawn ornaments."

The truth is, their property actually looks better now than when they moved in. They have professional landscapers who care for the yard, and they built a beautiful sunroom that overlooks the pool. There is nothing whatsoever tacky or low class about it. But that's just the way Tia Louisa is. My dad sometimes says that she thinks she's a gringo. Of course, he never says this to her face. That would be stupid. But after seeing Dad tonight, I'm thinking maybe he really is stupid.

I try to block the image of *that* woman from my mind, but I think it's been burned into my memory, like my brain got branded in one hot-white flash and the image of her will remain there forever. She's about Claire's height, about five-foot-eight, which makes her five inches taller than my mom. And she's very thin, whereas my mom is a little more rounded—not fat exactly, but she's definitely put on a few pounds over the last few years. This woman was not Hispanic, although she had a pretty good tan, which I'm guessing comes from a tanning bed. Her eyes were very blue and her hair was very blonde, but judging by her darker brows, I think she must have her hair lightened. And she was pretty.

Okay, it was kind of a harsh kind of pretty, like she tries too hard or uses too much makeup, but it would be hard not to admit she was pretty. I'm guessing she's in her thirties, but then I'm not good with grown-ups' ages. Still, I think she's younger than my mom, but that could have something to do with her clothes. She had on pale-blue velour sweats, low-cut pants that exposed a tan midriff, and a thin white shirt covered with a snug hoody. The whole outfit is something my mother would *never* wear—not in a million years. She doesn't even like it when *my* midriff shows. We've been arguing over that for several years now. And my mom's idea of "sweats" is loose, bulky, baggy, heavy clothes that would never fall into the category of "stylish." This woman was stylish.

I park my car in the steep driveway, remembering to put on my parking brake, and then dig through the shopping bags until I find a couple of things that I might possibly wear to school tomorrow.

Tia Louisa meets me at the door, giving me a somewhat restrained hug, which is just her style but comforting all the same.

She shakes her head. "This is too bad, Magdela. Come into the kitchen and tell me all about it."

I am relieved to hear that Tio Vito is at a meeting and won't be home for about an hour. And as I munch on their leftovers from dinner, I pour out my whole story, starting with my fight with Mom and finishing with the detailed description of the woman my dad is obviously seeing.

Tia Louisa refills my iced tea and lets out an exasperated sigh. "This is what I was afraid of."

"Afraid of?"

"Well, Rosa wouldn't go into much detail when I let her know I was aware of their problems."

I nod. "Yeah, she's been pretty tight-lipped about the whole thing. I don't get that. Do you think she even knows?"

"Oh, yes. I'm certain she knows. That would explain everything, Magdela."

"Everything?"

"Yes. The anger. Rosa has never been an angry person. But you told me she'd been nagging your father, picking fights, all of it. That's just the way a woman acts when her man is stepping out on her."

I wondered if she knew this from experience or if it's just something women innately understand. But as far as I know, Tio Vito has never cheated on her.

"Poor Rosa. I was worried that Roberto had another woman. I wish she could've told me. The poor woman needs to talk to someone. Keeping it all in will only make her want to explode."

"Well, she exploded tonight," I say. "On me."

"That's understandable. She has too many fireworks to hold in." Tia Louisa's brow creases, as if she's really thinking, trying to figure this whole thing out. "But I wonder why she's keeping it inside. Do you think she hopes they'll work all this out and get back together again before the family knows exactly what's happened?"

"She sure doesn't act like it," I say, "at least not when Dad's around. She really lets him have it."

"That's because she's so angry at him right now. But maybe she thought that if she could wait this thing out, he'd eventually come back to his senses, apologize to her, promise to never do this again, and then she would take him back. Do you think?"

"But you should see his place, Tia Louisa," I say. "It doesn't look like a temporary thing to me. I mean, it's really nice, and he's getting things to furnish it—even a big bed." I roll my eyes as I consider the ramifications of this. His back, my foot!

Tia Louisa frowns. "That's not good."

"And *that woman*."

"Really pretty, is she?"

I nod sadly.

"Well, your mother is going to have to face facts, Magdela. Sooner or later, the whole family will know what's going on. She might as well get it into the open now. And with Thanksgiving this week—by the way, are Marc and Elisa coming home? Your mother was a little sketchy about your family's plans. I would assume you're coming here like always, but then I realize that things are a little unsettled."

"Elisa isn't coming home. She has to work on Friday. Marc didn't sound sure. I think he's hoping his girlfriend will invite him home to meet her folks."

"So it's serious?"

I shrug. "I don't know, although he did want to bring her home for Christmas. I think both Elisa and Marc think this will all blow over by then." I sort of laugh. "In fact, I sort of thought the same thing—until tonight."

"It's possible we're reading too much into this," Tia Louisa says in an unconvincing tone. "Perhaps he just met this woman. Maybe he's not having an affair at all."

"I hope that's true. I really do. But I'd still have to wonder why he had her over tonight. He and Mom are still married, you know. And he told me he'd consider getting counseling. Yeah, right."

"Well, let's not jump to conclusions, Magdela."

Then she shows me to the guest suite, which I had assumed was only for adult guests.

"Oh, this is too nice," I tell her. "I can just stay in one of the boys' rooms."

She pats me on the back. "No, dear. I think you're in need of some special treatment tonight. You just make yourself at home." She nods to the beautiful bathroom that has marble everywhere, along with a big spa tub. "Take a bubble bath if it will make you feel better."

"Thanks," I tell her. "I might."

She looks at the shopping bag in my hand. "Did you have a chance to get what you needed before you left?"

"This is just something I happened to get at the mall today," I confess. "I don't have anything like a toothbrush or—"

"Look in that armoire," she says, pointing to a large antique piece. "I think you should find whatever you need. If you don't, just let me know. And if you don't mind, I think I will call it a night. I've been taking that new migraine medicine, and it seems to make me sleepy at the end of the day."

"Not at all," I tell her. "I hope it takes care of the headaches."

She nods. "So do I. Sleep well. Tomorrow is a whole new day."

So I indulge in a bubble bath, and then I watch TV for a while. And by the time I go to bed, I am feeling a little bit better. Okay, if all else fails with my parents, maybe Tia Louisa will adopt me!

eleven

I HAVE TO STOP BY MY HOUSE ON MONDAY MORNING TO PICK UP SOME homework (which is still unfinished) and some things I need for school. I'm hoping my mom will be at work, but that's unlikely since she doesn't usually go in until around nine. But if I'm lucky, she might be sleeping in. And it's not because I'm mad at her now. If anything, I guess I feel a little bit sorry for her—and hurt too. It hurts that (1) she's been so angry and mean to me, and (2) that she didn't tell me the truth about Dad.

Of course, it's possible she doesn't know the truth, in which case, I'm not sure what I should do. Do I tell her and risk having her go to pieces on me, or do I just keep my mouth shut and see what happens next? Also, it occurs to me that Tia Louisa could be right: That fling might be just a onetime thing with Dad. Maybe the woman is a neighbor who invited herself to dinner. Who knows? Still, I think it's more than that. Call it instinct or a gut feeling, but I think my dad's involved with that woman.

As it turns out, Mom's in the kitchen. She has on her old pink bathrobe and is drinking a cup of coffee as she flips through the morning paper. She barely looks up when I walk by. I consider just slinking past her, going to my room, grabbing my stuff, and making a quick and silent exit. But instead I pause for a moment and just look at her.

Her hair, which is longer than mine, is starting to thin and go gray, and it's lost most of its curl. The way it hangs limply over her shoulders makes her look much older than she is—almost haglike. Without any makeup, her face looks sallow and flat, and dark shadows show beneath her eyes. She really looks pretty pathetic, and the frumpy bathrobe and extra pounds don't help a bit.

"Are you okay?" I ask her.

She looks up, slightly surprised, and then just shrugs.

I take a deep breath. "I'm sorry for the stuff I said yesterday."

Her eyes seem to study me, as if she's trying to see whether I'm sincere. Finally, she says, "I'm sorry too."

"I just came to get some things for school."

"Meaning?"

"Huh?"

"Meaning are you getting things because you're not coming back?"

I frown. "I still don't get what you're asking."

"Well, last night you said you were going to live with your father. But then Louisa calls and tells me you're spending the night over there. I assume it was because your father wasn't home."

I don't miss that she's calling him my *father* now instead of my dad. And I'm guessing there is some significance in this slight change of terminology.

"So I'm wondering, Magdela, are you planning on moving out?"

"Do you want me to move out?"

She lets out a frustrated sigh. "Of course not, but I won't force you to stay here either. You're right. You're almost an adult. You should have a say in where you live."

I nod, somewhat satisfied. "Thanks."

"So where's it going to be?"

I look down at the floor.

"Magdela?"

"Here," I mumble.

"Really?" She seems surprised. "Are you sure?"

I consider Tia Louisa's beautiful house, not that she's invited me to stay. Awesome as it is, I think I'd be more comfortable in my own home. And despite everything, this still feels like it's my home—at least I hope it is. "Yeah," I tell her, "I'm sure."

She frowns now. "But what about your father? You were so dead set on moving in with him. What changed all that?"

I shrug and glance toward the window over the sink.

"Was he home last night?"

I don't want to answer her.

"Magdela?"

I consider lying but then wonder what good it will do. Like Tia Louisa said, this all has to come out into the open. Perhaps sooner is better. "Yes," I tell her, "he was home."

"But you didn't stay?" I feel her eyes on me now, studying me as if she actually does know something—or suspects it.

"No, I didn't."

"Why not?"

I look back at her now and realize that I should just say it, get it out. "He had a guest, Mom."

I see a flicker of hurt in her eyes, as if she really does know. "What kind of guest, Magdela?" Her words are calm and even now, but it's a forced kind of calm.

"A woman guest."

"Stephanie?" she asks without even blinking.

"I don't know." I stare at my mom, trying to determine if she might actually know this woman—the woman I saw last night. "I didn't stick around long enough to catch her name."

"Was she blonde?"

I nod.

"Tall and thin?"

I nod again.

"Pretty?"

"Yes. Do you know her?"

She kind of laughs. "Well, no, not actually. I know *of* her. She works with your dad. A coworker. A friend. You know."

"Is he having an affair with her?"

She kind of smiles now, but it's not a happy smile. "You'll have to ask him that, *mi hija*." Then she looks down and turns a page of the paper. "He's the only one who can answer that question."

"Right." I glance at the clock now. "I gotta go," I say quickly, "or I'll be late."

I grab my stuff and hurry to make it to school on time. But even though I am physically there, going to and from my classes, I might as well be sitting on the moon, because my brain is simply not working. All I can think is, *How can this be? How can my dad be having an affair? This is so wrong.*

I check my phone for messages at noon and am not surprised to see that my dad has called. Of course, he wants to straighten out this "unfortunate incident." "Can we meet for coffee?" he says. "I'll even get off work early. Four thirty at Java Hut? Let me know, okay?"

I don't call him back. I don't want to talk to him.

It feels freaky to switch gears like this. For a few weeks I have hated my mom, and now I hate my dad. What does this sort of thing do to your mind? Will it have a lasting effect? I tell myself that I should go directly home from school and catch up on my homework because I do have a sense that my grades are slipping. I imagine myself talking about it to Mr. Hurley, the academic counselor, trying to explain that it's really my parents' fault that I've pulled all Fs. "First I thought it was my mom," I would explain as he stroked his little gray moustache and frowned at me. "But then it was really my dad. And it's messing with my mind. It's starting to make my head hurt." Would he even get that? Would anyone?

"Are you okay?" Claire asks me on the way home from school on Wednesday. "You've been really quiet lately."

I've already filled her in on all the details of my parents. And while she was sympathetic, she was not surprised. "That's pretty much what I suspected," she told me after I poured out my sorry tale.

"Seriously?" I said. "You knew this and you didn't even tell me?"

"Well, it's the most obvious scenario. Man has an affair; woman gets left behind to pick up the pieces. You know. But it's not like I could tell you, especially when you were so convinced your dad was innocent. And to be honest, I guess I hoped he was. I mean, I've always liked your dad."

"Do you now?"

She shrugs. "I don't know. I guess, for your sake, I'm mad at him. But he's probably still a nice guy."

"A nice guy?"

"Oh, I don't know. But eventually you'll have to forgive him, you know?"

"Forgive him?"

"I know it's hard to imagine. It took me years to forgive my dad."

"And you actually did?"

"Yeah. We're supposed to forgive, Maggie. Don't you ever listen to the sermons and stuff? God forgave us; we forgive others. You've probably been hearing that since you were in diapers."

I nod. "Yeah, yeah, I know." But I'm thinking it's going to take a serious miracle—I mean, God will have to totally intervene—for me to be able to forgive Dad. Crud, I can't even talk to him right now.

"Do you work today?" she asks as she pulls up in front of my house.

"Yeah, but not tomorrow."

"Right. Well, have a good Thanksgiving," she says. "Call me on Friday. Maybe we can do something."

"Thanks."

"At least you get to see Ned today," she says brightly.

I nod. "Yeah, if he's there."

"I can't wait to hear how that's going."

I smile and wave, hoping that I look more cheerful than I feel. I know my gloominess is a drag for her. I have to try harder to at least *look* happy. True, at least I might see Ned tonight. That's something.

I'm pleased to see that Ned is at work. We visit pleasantly during lulls, of which there are many. It seems not too many people go out to eat the night before Thanksgiving.

"I don't know why I even open sometimes," my aunt complains as she glances around the mostly deserted dining room and rubs her temples with her forefingers.

"A migraine?" I ask.

"Hopefully not." She looks at her watch. "If it doesn't pick up, we might as well start to close early. Maybe eight thirty. Do you want to inform the kitchen?"

As it turns out, we do close early. And as I'm getting my coat, Ned asks me if I want to get a cup of coffee. "There's a Starbucks just down the street."

"Sure," I say. "That sounds good."

So we walk together, and I tell myself that this is almost like a date. Okay, maybe it's just coworkers going out for coffee, but I can still enjoy it. The air is really crisp and cold, and Ned thinks it could actually snow.

"This time of year?" I say skeptically.

"It's happened before."

"Not that I can remember."

"I remember snow on Thanksgiving one year," he persists.

"No way," I challenge. "On Thanksgiving? I've lived here all my life, and I don't remember that."

"Maybe you were too little," he teases.

"You're not that much older than me," I insist. "I'll be eighteen in February."

"A grown woman?" But I hear the lightness in his voice, as if he still thinks I'm a little girl.

We order our coffee and go sit down. Not unlike the restaurant, this place is dead too. "Where is everyone?" I say as I glance around at the empty tables.

"Home, stuffing their turkeys?"

I laugh. "You don't stuff turkeys the night before, silly."

"Oh."

"What are you doing for Thanksgiving?" I ask.

"Sleeping in."

"I mean after that."

"Nothing."

"Not spending time with family? Eating too much turkey? Going into a tryptophan-induced coma in front of a football game?"

He smiles. "No, as wonderful as that sounds, I am not."

"Really?" I frown now. "That seems kind of sad."

He nods. "Yeah, it does, doesn't it? Do you feel sorry for me? That I'm all alone in the world? No family to go home to?"

"Really? You really don't have any family?" With all my extended family, not just on my mom's side in this town but also where my dad comes from, a few hours from here, I find this impossible to even imagine.

"My parents split up a few years ago," he says. "They both remarried, and my dad moved to Arizona, and my mom and her new husband have been doing a lot of traveling. Right now, they're in Cancun, I think it is, or maybe it's Thailand. I'm not sure."

"Siblings?"

"A sister in Boston."

"Aunts, uncles, grandparents?"

"Here and there. But we've never been really close. My dad was military, and we moved around a lot. We never had time to do the family stuff."

I shake my head. "That is so sad."

"Maybe. But only around the holidays. And then I hear some of my friends complaining about how awful their holidays are and how everyone gets into these big fights, and I think, *Hey, maybe I'm lucky*. I'm free. I can come and go as I please."

"Maybe." I consider this. "But I still think it's sad."

"Well, I figure I can always marry into a big, happy family." He winks at me. "Like yours, for instance. I already know that your aunt Louisa has all kinds of relatives. What's your family like?"

Okay, now I'm feeling seriously torn. On one hand, he's just talked about marrying into a big, happy family (I know he's probably just kidding), but now he wants to know about my family—like we're so happy.

I start by telling him about my sister and brother, and how we do have a lot of extended family, and how birthdays, holidays, weddings, whatever, always turn into a big celebration. "And the food is usually good."

He smiles and rubs his hands together. "You're tempting me, Maggie. Are you already spoken for? I've heard that some Latino families still believe in arranged marriages. Maybe I should put in a word to Eduardo."

I laugh. "Well, wait until you hear the whole story. It gets worse." So then I tell about my parents, but not with all the details. In fact, I probably make it sound more positive than it really is.

"That's a bummer," he says.

"I know."

"Parents don't realize how this messes up our lives."

"I know."

"They think just because we're all grown-up, or nearly grown-up, that it doesn't matter. But then you get stuck trying to figure out what to do for the holidays and weddings, like my sister when she got married. Who sits where? And do you invite them both and risk having a big scene?"

"I haven't even considered that."

"There's all kinds of things, like when kids come. I guess that's okay when they get tons of presents from like four sets of grandparents. But it seems like it would be confusing too."

I nod. "Yeah. Like what would you call them?"

"Grandma One, Grandma Two, and so on."

We talk some more, and it occurs to me that my parents have set me up for all kinds of problems I haven't even begun to think about.

"Sorry," he says finally.

"For what?"

"I didn't mean to depress you with all my parental divorce talk."

"You've given me things to consider."

"Well, you'll get through this, Maggie. We all survive."

Then we walk back to our cars, and Ned waits to make sure I'm safely in mine—such a gentleman—and we both drive away. But as I'm driving, it occurs to me that I should've invited Ned to have Thanksgiving with our family. I'm sure Tia Louisa wouldn't mind. Maybe I can give her a call in the morning.

twelve

IT FEELS WEIRD WHEN IT'S JUST MOM AND ME DRIVING OVER TO TIA Louisa's the next day, but I try to act normal, especially since Mom seems a little uptight, and I even carry on a conversation with her.

"So this is a guy you work with?" she asks as she turns to go up the hill.

"Yes. He doesn't have any family close to here, and Tia Louisa said it was fine for him to come. He already knows her and Vito and Eduardo and I don't know who else, so he's kind of like family."

"Is he Hispanic?"

I laugh. "No way. And his last name is Schlamowski."

"Good grief, what a name."

"Anyway, I think he was relieved to have a place to go. You know, he works to put himself through college. His parents are barely helping him, and his mom even married this really rich guy. But Ned doesn't want to take money from him because it would make his real dad feel bad."

"He sounds like a thoughtful young man." Then she turns and looks at me curiously. "You're not interested in him, are you, Maggie?"

"No," I say quickly. "He's just a good friend."

"Oh, good. How old is he anyway?"

"Just twenty."

She nods without commenting. But I think I can see the wheels in her head turning. She's probably thinking that her youngest daughter better not get involved with someone that old. I'm tempted to remind her that I'll be eighteen before long, but then I figure, Why rock her boat? Especially today, when it probably feels like it's already sinking.

The dinner goes relatively smoothly. I think Ned feels pretty much at home. He really does know a fair number of my relatives. Even Brad and Andy have met him before. And the other cousins make him feel right at home. Everyone thinks he's here because of the connection with Louisa and Eduardo and the restaurant, so I don't feel any pressure to explain why he is here or that I was the one who actually invited him.

After dinner, the older adults mingle in the great room upstairs. The men, naturally, gravitate to the football game, and the women go off to the sunroom. The rest of us go downstairs to play pool and video games, pausing now and then to check on the game, which is so boring that I'm pretty sure my uncles must all be snoring by now.

Once again, Ned fits in just fine. And even though I'm still the youngest, it seems like they're treating me more like one of the gang, like maybe they think I finally grew up. Or maybe they're just being sympathetic because by now everyone is well aware that my dad has left my mom.

No one really discusses it, except in hushed whispers, especially whenever Mom or I are within earshot. But I know they are thinking about it, probably feeling sorry for us and curious as to what the "rest of the story" is. Maybe the women are up there grilling Mom right now. I try not to think about that as I concentrate on getting the two ball into the corner pocket.

Ned leaves before anyone else, excusing himself to "go study" since it's not long until finals and he's taking some hard classes this term. But he thanks me for inviting him and says he'll see me at work tomorrow. After that, the other cousins start making plans—some to go out partying, I'm sure—and the crowd begins to break up.

Mom seems relieved to go. I'm sure she's tired of answering questions. I'm curious as to how she answered them since she still hasn't come right out and said that Dad is definitely having an affair. She keeps telling me to go ask *him* if I want to get to the bottom of it. But despite the messages he's left asking to meet with me, I am still unwilling to talk. However, curiosity may eventually win out. I realize now that I'd feel bad to blame him for cheating on Mom all this time if he is, in fact, innocent—although it seems unlikely. Still, I've been wrong before. I was wrong—or I think I was—to be totally blaming Mom early on.

I finally call my dad the next day, leaving him a message that I'll meet him for coffee on Sunday, if that works for him. "After church," I say as if giving him a hint, like some people still go to church. Okay, maybe I don't listen so well in church, and maybe I'm not really living like much of a Christian, but my dad doesn't have to know everything.

The next couple of shifts at work are actually fun. The restaurant is busier than ever. "The after-shopping crowd," my aunt explains. "Everyone's in great spirits for the holidays. We'll be busy like this right up until Christmas." I can tell this makes her happy, almost like those old cartoons where you see the dollar signs in the characters' eyes. But then, in her defense, I think it's more than the money. I think she enjoys the energy, the feeling of good cheer, the music, the food, well, everything about the restaurant. And, more and more, I think I do too.

Ned and I continue to chat, and I can tell we are getting closer. Okay, it might be "just as friends," but that's okay. He makes a good friend, and he's easy to look at too. Who knows what might develop on down the line. It's not like I'm in any hurry to run off and elope with him, although I do imagine it at times. Not to make it seem that I've changed my opinion on marriage—the jury is still out on that—but sometimes (in my daydreams) I imagine Ned and myself living happily together (as man and wife) and how our home would look and what it would feel like to be loved and protected by him. And I have to say, it's not bad.

When it's time to meet Dad on Sunday, I wonder if I made a mistake. Am I really ready to talk to him? I feel slightly sick as I park in front of Java Hut. My dad's Explorer is already here, parked on the other side of the street. I brace myself as I go through the door, spying my dad over by the window, the same table we sat at last time—last time, when I was vowing my allegiance and support of him, so certain that my mom was the witch, the evil cause behind their breakup. Oh, how the tables can turn. I warn myself to be fair—I haven't heard the whole story yet.

Dad has already ordered for me—a mocha like I usually have—but it irritates me and makes me want to say that I'd really prefer an espresso, although I've never even tasted an espresso. Claire says they're like coffee on steroids. I sit down and just look at him.

"How are you doing, Magpie?"

I shrug. "I've been better."

"Yeah, I know." He nods to the coffee. "I got your favorite."

"Thanks," I say in a flat voice without touching the mug.

"We need to talk."

I nod without speaking and still don't touch the mug.

"I know that you must have some questions, about Stephanie, I mean."

So it actually *was* Stephanie—not that there was really any question. Mom seemed pretty certain.

"I'm sure you were shocked to see, well, a woman in my apartment. But I can explain."

I look evenly at him. I want to say, "Fine, why don't you?" But I just sit there. To my surprise, it doesn't bother me in the least to see him uncomfortable like that. I want to make him squirm.

"Stephanie works with me." He waits, like I'm going to say something, which I am not. "We've been friends, well, for some time."

"Friends?" I repeat the word, making my tone suggest that perhaps they are more than just friends.

"Yes. She's a nice person, Maggie. I think you'd like her."

I can feel my eyes now. It's like there is fire behind them, and I have a feeling they look a lot like Mom's when she's starting to fume. But I remain calm.

"I never meant for this to happen," he says with a sad expression. "Some things are hard to understand, I mean, how they happen. But I want you to know that I never planned it, never actually thought to myself that I would really do something, you know?"

I shake my head. "No, I don't know. Why don't you explain?"

"Well, it's not like I got out of bed one morning and said to myself, 'I think I'll get involved with someone.' It just wasn't like that, premeditated, you know."

"So what was it, Dad? Did she sneak up on you in the copy room, jump you from behind, and then just take you?"

Dad looks slightly amused, although I didn't mean to be funny. "No, it wasn't like that either."

"What was it like?"

"We fell in love."

Okay, gag me! Seriously, this makes me sick, but I try to keep my face composed. I really do want to get to the bottom of this. Even if it does remind me of the time our dog Shaniko ate a battery from one of my toys (my fault, since I think I fed it to him) and I had to go out in the backyard and wait for him to do his "job" and then I had to use a stick to dig through the pile in order to see if the battery was in there. Fortunately, it was or we would've had to take him to the vet. That dog is long gone now, but getting to the bottom of my dad's story feels sickeningly similar to that whole fiasco.

"I know you're probably thinking that it's wrong, that I should love only your mother. And I can understand that, honey. Like I said, I didn't exactly plan this. But being with Stephanie, well . . ." He looks over my shoulder, as if he sees something there besides the wall. "She makes me feel alive again and like I want to get up in the morning, and she really understands me, and we're just in love. How else can I explain it?"

"Are you having an affair?"

He puts his hand over his mouth, partially covering what I now think is a very ugly goatee. In fact, I think it makes him look like the devil. Maybe he is.

"Are you, Dad?" I glare at him. "Are you sleeping with her?" My voice has grown louder, and the couple at the nearest table looks our way. But I don't care.

Now he looks away, but judging by his expression, I have my answer.

"So you have been cheating on Mom." I say the ugly words for him. "How long has it been going on, Dad? How long have you been cheating on Mom?"

His cheeks are getting flushed, and he looks slightly alarmed now, like this conversation is going too far, too fast, and it's ready to derail him any moment. He looks at me in that way—the way that asks me if I'll just let this go, just understand, just be his gullible little Magpie, the daughter who totally adores him and accepts him and believes whatever he wants her to believe. Well, those days are gone, Dad!

"How long has this been going on?" I repeat my question since he seems to have forgotten it.

He clears his throat. "Well, Stephanie and I have been seeing each other for a few months now."

"A few months?" My voice is really loud. "You've been having an affair with this woman for a few months? When did Mom find out anyway?"

"Can you keep it down?" He glances around. "There are other people here, you know."

"Fine." I lower my voice, but the damage is done. I think everyone in here knows that my dad's been cheating on my mom, and I don't care. I don't care that this is his favorite coffee shop and he may not want to show his face in here again. Or maybe he's already brought Stephanie here. Maybe they know.

"Your mom found out in September."

I nod knowingly. "About the same time she started losing it? The same time she started getting grumpy, getting on your case, acting like she was living in a state of continual hormonal meltdown? Well, doesn't that figure."

"Of course, she was upset. You can't blame her."

"Blame her?" I challenge him. "You saw me blaming her. You saw me making her out to be the demon woman, the one who drove you from our home. And you just let me. You never admitted—"

"There are two sides to this, Magdela," he says in a firm tone. "You haven't heard everything yet."

"Yeah, right. Mom falls apart when she learns you're cheating on her, and she's to blame. You bet." I just shake my head in disgust. "But I want to know something. Why didn't she make you leave in September when she found out? Why did she let you stay?"

"We thought we could work it out."

Now I soften just a little. "Why can't you, Dad?" I plead with him. "Why can't you work it out?" As I wait for him to answer, it occurs to me that the reason my mom let him stay, the reason she thought they could work this out, was probably because she still loved him. She probably still does. "I'll bet she would forgive you, Dad. Did you ask her?"

He still doesn't answer, but I persist.

"Did you give her that chance, Dad? Did you ask her to forgive you? Did you ask her to go for counseling with you?"

He just shakes his head.

"Why not?"

Now he looks evenly at me, and more than ever, he seems like a stranger to me. It's like something in his eyes is different, like I don't know this man anymore. But I ask him again. "Why not, Dad?"

"Because I don't want to. Because it's over, Maggie."

I look down at my untouched mocha, thankful that I didn't drink a drop of this man's poison, and then I stand up. "I don't want to have anything to do with you, Dad," I tell him evenly. "As far as I'm concerned, you are dead." Then I walk out, get in my car, and drive away.

thirteen

DESPITE MY TOUGH TALK, MY HEART IS BROKEN. AND AS MUCH AS I HATE him, I still don't know what to do about certain things—things like memories, like when he taught me to ride a bike and wouldn't give up until I got it, or the time he bought me the exact dress I wanted (the one Mom had told me was too expensive) for my first formal dance. How do you wipe those memories away? How do you delete entire portions of your life?

I end up following my mom's example, the very thing that had me undone just a month ago, and I remove all traces of my dad from my room, including team photos taken during the years when Dad coached our soccer team. I even place the formal dress in a box and shove it to the back of my closet. I just don't want to be reminded of him anymore.

Mom knows that something is wrong with me. I can see it in her eyes when we meet on the stairs or in the kitchen, coming and going our separate ways. And I can tell by the way she talks to me, like there's this question in her voice. Of course, she has no idea that I met with Dad or that I know about *the affair*. But she eventually corners me and makes her inquiry.

I'm barely through the door after a busy night at work, and all I want to do is kick off my shoes and veg out in front of the boob tube to block it all out, maybe watch the latest reality show that Claire was telling me about today. I'm grabbing a soda from the fridge when Mom comes into the kitchen.

"Are you okay, Maggie?"

"What do you mean?" I pop open the can and take a swig.

"You've just seemed pretty quiet the past couple of days, and I thought we'd made some progress. We were starting to talk again, and it felt good. Have I done something to offend you?" Her expression is so sweet and sincere just now that it makes me want to cry.

"No, Mom," I say quickly. "It's not you. Not at all. The furthest thing from it."

She sits down on the stool by the counter as if this is going to take more than just a minute or two. "Well, what then, Maggie? Anything you can tell me about? Boy trouble?"

I kind of laugh. "Not exactly." Then I study her for a moment, wondering if she's ready to hear this. In a way, she seems stronger than she was a few weeks ago, like maybe she's moving on now. "It's more like *man* trouble," I tell her, pulling out a stool for myself. I sit down, preparing myself for what will probably be an uncomfortable conversation and hoping it will be brief.

Her brows lift. "You mean Ned? Are you and Ned getting involved?"

"No, Mom." Now this kind of irritates me. What if Ned and I were involved? Would it really be that bad? I realize he's older, out of high school, in college. But it won't be long until I'm in the same place. Can't she see that? I'm not exactly a baby anymore.

"Well, what kind of man trouble are you having, Magdela? You know, that's not exactly the kind of thing a mother wants to hear from her daughter."

"It's *your* man," I tell her, showing my exasperation.

She nods a bit stiffly. "Oh."

"I talked to him on Sunday."

She puts her elbows on the countertop, resting her chin on her folded hands, almost as if she's bracing herself. "And?"

"And he admitted to having an affair with Stephanie."

Mom presses her lips together, trying to appear, I'm sure, as if this isn't any big surprise. And yet she looks hurt too. And I almost get the feeling that she's hearing this news for the first time, although I know that's not really the case.

"And I asked him if he'd asked you to forgive him, if he'd considered getting help and patching things up."

Now Mom sits up straighter, looking slightly hopeful. "And?"

"He doesn't want to."

"Oh." Her chin quivers, ever so slightly, and it reminds me of a little girl, and suddenly I just want to hug her.

"I'm sorry, Mom."

She shakes her head. "No, it's okay, Maggie. I suspected that might be the situation."

"You mean with Stephanie?"

"Yes. So that's it then? He plans to stay with—with her then?"

"Yeah, it looks that way."

Her face looks very pale now, but she just slowly nods and then stands up, placing her hands on the counter as if to steady herself. "Well, I can't say I'm not a little surprised. He told me this was just a phase, like a midlife crisis, you know. He thought it would end soon."

"He didn't sound like that to me."

Now she studies me very closely. "Are you certain of this, Magdela? Are you absolutely sure? Please don't spare my feelings.

I need to know. This will help me make some decisions and move on with my life. I do not want to be stuck in limbo, stupidly thinking that if I wait long enough he'll come around. Do you understand what I'm saying? I *need* to know."

"He said he's in love with her, Mom."

"Thank you, Maggie. Thank you for your honesty." She takes in a deep breath. "I think I'll go to bed now. I have a closing in the morning."

"Are you okay, Mom?" I ask as she goes toward the stairs.

"I'm fine, Maggie." But her voice sounds thin and frail and anything but fine. "Good night."

And when I go to my room, after watching the last twenty minutes of what turns out to be a totally lame reality show, I hear my mom. She is quietly crying in her room. I stand by her door for a couple of minutes, unsure as to whether I should go in. Then I think about what I would want in a similar situation, if my heart were breaking like hers is, and I suspect I'd want to be alone—at least for a while. So I don't knock on the door like I want to. I just go to my room and cry too.

For the next two weeks, it doesn't seem the least bit like December in our house. Normally, my mom would have decorated every square inch of the place on the inside, and Dad would've hung lights on the outside. Our tree would be up in the living room, Mom's favorite Latino Christmas music would be playing, and she would have a good start on her Christmas baking, starting with Mexican wedding cakes that she would wrap and store in the freezer. But not this year.

I try to pretend I don't mind. Since I spend most of my evenings working and the others trying to stay caught up on homework, it's not that big of a deal. But I do warn Elisa and Marc about the Scrooge state of our home. "Don't expect much. It looks like it's going to be a bleak Christmas," I tell them in an e-mail. They're both aware of our dad's affair by now. Marc, of course, says he knew it all along. Elisa, like me, is a little surprised. "It seems out of character," she wrote back to me. "Does this mean he's not a Christian anymore?" Well, I didn't know how to answer that, but I told her she might want to ask him. I also told her that I've completely written him off, that I no longer consider him my dad. "You can't do that," she wrote back. "Just because they're splitting up doesn't mean he's not your dad." I didn't even respond to that in my next e-mail. I simply told her that Mom was in pain and that she needed our support more than ever right now.

Finally, it's the beginning of Christmas break, and our gloomy house is seriously bugging me, so I get an idea. I call Claire and ask her if she wants to help me cheer up my mom.

"What do you have in mind? A trip to Nevada for a quickie divorce?"

I sort of laugh. "No. I thought we could decorate my house for Christmas. It's so depressing around here. And Marc will be home on Saturday, and then Elisa a few days after that."

"That's a great idea, Maggie!"

So the next day, Claire and I make several trips to the attic, hauling down carton after carton of Mom's carefully organized Christmas stuff. I try to remember where she likes things, and then Claire and I go to work. It's actually pretty fun, and by the end of the day, it looks way better. I even put on Mom's favorite Christmas CDs.

"Too bad we didn't have time to make cookies," Claire says as she gets ready to leave.

"Well, maybe this will inspire my mom," I say. "Thanks so much for the help."

"Let me know what she thinks."

When Mom comes home, she seems pretty surprised. She walks through the house and checks out our handiwork. Okay, it sort of hurts my feelings when she changes a couple of the decorations around, like we didn't get it quite right, but I don't say anything—after all, this is her territory, not mine. But then she sits down on the couch directly across from the fireplace, which I happen to think we did a pretty good decorating job on, and she begins to cry.

I don't know what to do. Finally, I tell her I'm sorry. "I guess we shouldn't have done this," I say, feeling defensive and ready to speak my mind.

"No, honey," she says, looking at me with wet eyes. "It's wonderful. It's sweet. But it just makes me sad." She starts crying again. "This will be our first Christmas, you know . . ."

Then I put my arms around her and hug her. "Yeah, I know. But we can't just skip it, can we? I mean, it's still Christmas whether Dad is around or not. And Elisa and Marc will be here, and . . ." I begin crying too.

"I'm sorry, Maggie," she says when she sees my tears. "I really do appreciate this. And you're right. We can't skip Christmas just because your father is a jerk."

I nod. "That's right. And you know what? I hope he feels bad, you know, when he realizes we're all over here having a good time and he doesn't even have us anymore. That would serve him right."

She smiles. "Yes, it would. A friend at work was just telling me that very same thing. She said the best revenge is to live well. And maybe that's just what we'll do, Maggie." She stands up now, pulling me to my feet. "And tonight we'll bake cookies!"

"All right!"

And that's just what we do. And we talk about how it will be when Elisa and Marc and his new girlfriend, Liz, arrive, and how we'll invite some family and friends over for Christmas Eve, and how we'll have a good time at Tia Louisa's house on Christmas Day. And I try to imagine my dad standing out in the cold, his nose pressed against the front window as he watches us all laughing and having a good time. Okay, I realize that won't really happen, but the image makes me feel better. I really do want him to suffer.

"I can get a tree tomorrow," I tell Mom as we're finishing up in the kitchen. "I saw a place near Casa del Sol that has them marked down to half price. I could pick one up before work and tie it to my roof."

"That's a great idea, Maggie. We must have a tree."

So the next day, I go to work a little early to pick out a tree. But I must admit to feeling a little blue as I walk around the parking lot looking at trees that have about as much Christmas cheer as I do at the moment. Normally, I would be thrilled to see the snow-flakes that are just beginning to swirl in the freezing wind, but mostly I feel cold—cold and lonely and sad. This isn't how getting a Christmas tree should feel.

I try not to remember when Dad would take us kids to get a tree at the U-Cut place just outside of town. We'd all pile onto a horse-drawn wagon, careful not to spill our free cups of hot cocoa as we rode out to where the Christmas trees grew in long neat rows. Everything smelled so sweet and fresh and piney, and we'd take forever to find just the right tree. But Dad never complained. "We have to get the perfect one," he'd say as we tromped around. *Don't think about it,* I tell myself. *Let the memories go. Dad is dead.*

"Hey, Maggie!" calls a voice.

I look over to see Ned's bright-green vintage Volkswagen bug on the side of the street, behind my car. His head, topped in a brightly striped ski hat, the kind with ear flaps and a tassel on top, is sticking out the open window as he wildly waves at me.

I wave back, smiling at his clownish appearance. "Hi, Ned!"

"Whatcha doing?"

"Getting a tree."

"Need some help?"

"Yes!" I yell loudly to be heard above the semitruck that's whizzing by him. "I do!"

So he hops out of his car and comes over. "So," he says in an official sort of way, "what kind of a tree are we looking for today?"

I shrug. "I'm not sure I can find what I'm looking for. I mean, they're pretty sad-looking, don't you think?"

"Oh, I don't know about that." He reaches for a tree that's about his height and stands it up straight so we can see it better. One side is flattened and the top is slightly bent.

I touch a branch, and dry needles cascade to the ground. "Looks like a disaster just waiting to happen."

He nods, letting the tree fall back to the wood support it was leaning on. "Definitely not good."

We walk around looking at a few more, and I begin telling him about how I was having this flashback to the days when we kids used to get fresh beautiful trees with my dad at the tree farm.

"Hey, I've heard about that place," he says with interest. "It sounds like fun."

"Yeah," I say sadly, "it was."

"Why can't it still be?"

I consider this. "Well, I'm sure it is for some people, but I don't think I could handle driving out there by myself and getting a tree. Seems kind of pathetic, don't you think?"

"Why don't we go together?"

"Really?"

"Yeah. I had my last final today, and I'm pretty free for the next couple of weeks. My roommate invited me to go snowboarding, but I can't afford it. So I'll probably just be sleeping in and feeling sorry for myself anyway. Want to go in the morning? That gives us plenty of time to be back at work."

"That sounds great!"

And so I'm feeling pretty stoked as I work my shift tonight, thinking about how cool it will be to go with Ned to the tree farm, how it will be almost like a date—although I will drive, since my car has a bigger roof to tie the tree onto—but it will be just the two of us, together for several hours. And because I'm feeling so happy, I'm probably being extra friendly and cheerful to our customers. I'm not sure if it's just me, but it seems like everyone is in an especially jolly mood tonight. Maybe it's the real spirit of Christmas.

I smile to myself as I brush a white tablecloth clean, careful not to get crumbs on the chairs, and then I quickly but meticulously reset the table, taking a moment to adjust the red roses with the tiny pine bough (my aunt's sophisticated Christmas touch), and then return for the party of four who will be sitting there.

"Right this way, please," I tell them as I lead them to the table, help them get seated, fill their water glasses, and take their beverage orders. "And your waiter tonight will be Ned," I say as I see Ned coming their way. I want to add, "and he's the cutest waiter here," but of course, I control myself.

"I think you might be the best hostess we've ever had," Tia Louisa tells me as the evening rush begins to slow down.

"Thanks," I reply. This is high praise coming from my aunt. "I really do love working here."

She smiles. "That's probably why you're doing such a good job, then. When you love what you do, people notice."

I consider her words as I'm driving home and decide she must be right. I wonder how she got so smart about these things, although I suspect it comes with age and experience. It makes sense that people should get smarter over time—well, most people anyway. Unfortunately, my dad isn't one of them. He seems to have only gotten stupider with age. Or maybe he's reverted back to his adolescence.

That's when I see the bitter irony of it: He's acting like a teenager and, as a result, I'm having to grow up and go to work and do things like decorate our house for Christmas and get our family a Christmas tree. I have to admit these things are kind of fun, and the idea of going with Ned tomorrow is certainly no hardship, but it hits me that maybe I'm not just *pretending* to be a grown-up anymore—maybe I really am growing up. Just the thought of this makes me sit up a little straighter in my car, and it even makes me drive more carefully—well, that and the snow that's beginning to accumulate on the road. I'm not used to driving in these conditions.

fourteen

THE WORLD OUTSIDE IS WHITE AND BEAUTIFUL WHEN I GET UP THE NEXT morning. Really amazing! Even though I'm only going tree hunting, I try on several combinations of clothes until I decide on my favorite jeans and burgundy Gap sweater, which look great with this knitted scarf-and-hat set that Claire gave me for my birthday last year. Of course, I wear my snow boots and parka and even remember to stuff mittens in my pockets.

The plan is to meet at my house (I figured this was a good way to show Ned where I live, just in case) and try to be on the road by ten since it's about a forty-minute drive to the tree farm. That'll give us at least two hours to hunt down the perfect tree, grab a bite to eat, and get back here without being late to work.

Ned arrives just before ten. I invite him inside and ask if he wants a cup of coffee to take.

"Sounds great," he says. I pull out a couple of travel mugs and we're set.

"I'm not that experienced at driving on snow," I admit as we go outside.

"Want me to drive? I've driven on snow a lot. I snowboarded all through high school and drove up to the mountains almost every weekend."

I consider this. My dad has a strict policy: "No one drives your car but you, Magdela." But then, my dad's not exactly around to enforce this rule anymore. I look at my '96 Neon, which I dearly love, and imagine how it would look if it slid off the road and hit something.

"Sure," I tell him, "if you're really good on the snow."

"Yeah," he assures me. "Trust me, I've never wrecked yet."

Just the idea of wrecking is a little unnerving. I buckle my seat belt, but as I observe Ned's careful driving, I begin to relax. This is going to be okay.

"Can you believe this snow?" I say as I look at the blanket of white. "It's so beautiful. I hope it sticks around until Christmas."

"I heard there's another storm system coming in a few days," he says as he gets onto the highway that leads out of town. "Could mean more snow."

"Cool." I sip my coffee and think that today is going to be perfect.

We talk all the way to the tree farm. Ned tells me about his mom and her husband and how they invited him to meet them in Hawaii for Christmas. "Mike has a condo in Maui," he continues, "right on the beach."

"Man, everyone else has all the luck. My friend Claire just told me that her parents are going to the Caribbean for Christmas break. Life is so unfair."

"I think it all balances out eventually."

"So are you going to go then? To Maui?"

"I gotta admit, it sounds really tempting." He sighs. "But the thing is, my dad and his wife also have invited me to come stay at their place for Christmas."

"Oh. So are you going there then?"

He just shakes his head. "I don't think so. It's like whichever one I choose, the other one's going to be mad. I'm like a man without a country—or a home, for that matter."

"That's tough."

"Yep."

"If it were me, I'd go to Maui."

"What if it was your dad and his girlfriend inviting you?"

"Oh." I frown. "That would be different. I would definitely not go to Maui."

"See what I mean? It's complicated."

"Well, it won't be for me," I tell him, "because as far as I'm concerned, my dad and his bimbo do not exist. I would never be tempted to spend a holiday or even a few minutes with them."

"Don't be so quick to write him off, Maggie."

"Why not?" I turn and look at Ned, reassured to see that he's really focusing on the road. "My dad's a total jerk. He cheated on my mom. He broke her heart. He's hurting our entire family. I don't see why I shouldn't write him off."

"Yeah, I can understand how you feel that way—in the beginning. But he's still your dad. It's pretty hard to pretend like he doesn't exist. Like, what if you needed him for something?"

"Like what?" I demand. "What could I possibly need from that man?"

"A kidney?" Ned chuckles, and I start to laugh.

"Yeah, right."

"You never know, Maggie."

"Well, it'll be a snowy day like this down under if I ever go begging for one of Dad's kidneys. I think I'd rather die."

Ned changes the subject after that, and before I know it, we are there. I'm a little surprised at how expensive these trees are—nearly three times what I would've paid at the crummy tree lot—*but*, I tell myself as I shell out the cash, *this is worth it.*

Ned carries the saw, and we go get our "free" hot cocoas and wander around for a while as we wait for the next wagon to return. Then we pile on, along with a family of two parents and three little girls and an older couple, and ride on up to where the trees are growing.

"It's like Currier and Ives," says the older woman as her husband takes a picture of the big red barn with his camera. The little girls giggle and roll around in the hay behind us, just the way my sister and brother and I used to do, until the youngest girl gets a candy cane stuck in her hair and the other two quietly try to undo it before the parents notice.

The wagon stops, and Ned helps me get out—so polite—and then we walk around examining the trees.

"They're all so pretty," I say at first. "It probably doesn't matter which one we choose." But as I look more carefully, I realize there are a few differences. Some are taller and thinner, some are full and stout. But I know that my mom likes a tree that's about six feet tall and full. So I tell Ned this is what we're looking for, and after nearly an hour, we find the "perfect" tree. Ned cuts it down and we carry it back to the wagon stop.

"It smells so good," I say as we walk through the snow.

"I think I'm going to be smelling it all day. I've got the pitchy end."

"Sorry," I tell him. "Do you want to switch?"

"No. I like the smell. They should bottle it as cologne."

I laugh. "Eau de Pine Tree?"

We ride the wagon back to the parking lot, get the tree securely tied onto my roof, and drive back the way we came.

"How about getting lunch at that little café we saw along the way?" Ned suggests.

"Okay," I say. I don't tell him that it's the same place Dad used to take us kids to and that it's probably going to take me down memory lane again.

But as we park and go inside, I remind myself that today is the making of a brand-new memory. Perhaps thinking of how Ned and I came up here to get a tree together will block out all the memories that include my dad.

I insist on treating for lunch since we came out here for my sake in the first place. Ned is reluctant but finally gives in, saying, "Okay, but I get the next one."

I smile and agree, wondering, *Does this mean there will be a next one?*

Then Ned carefully drives us back home. But as he pulls my car into the driveway, I see an all-too-familiar Explorer pulling up right behind us. I quickly get out of the car, but not fast enough for my dad to miss the fact that Ned, not me, is the driver.

"Magdela," he calls as he comes toward us, a frown on his face. "What are you doing?"

I glare at him. "What does it look like I'm doing?"

He looks at Ned as he climbs from the car. "Who is this?"

I make a halfhearted introduction, and Ned reaches out to shake my dad's hand, which my dad offers in a reluctant way. I want to slap him.

"So why is someone else driving your car, Magdela?" He is using his fatherly voice now, trying to appear as if he's the authority here.

I just shrug. "Because it's snowy and I haven't had that much experience—"

"Did you go all the way to the tree farm?" my dad demands as he sees the tag on the tree. "In this weather?"

"Duh." I glance toward the house now.

"It wasn't that bad," says Ned in a congenial way.

But my father ignores him, turning to me instead. "You know my rule about the car, Magdela."

"I didn't know that your rules applied anymore—I mean once you started breaking them yourself." Then I turn and start untying the tree. Ned helps me, and my dad just stands there watching us.

We have the tree down now. "Let's shake the snow off and then take it to the porch," I tell Ned, ignoring my father.

Soon we have the tree on the porch, and my father is still standing in the driveway.

"I'm going inside," I say to Ned. "You want to come in and have a soda?"

"Sure." He turns to my father and waves. "Nice to meet you, sir."

"You didn't have to be so nice," I tell Ned once we're inside and the door is closed.

"Well, he's not really the enemy, Maggie."

"Yeah, right."

"Okay, I know it feels that way to you, but he's not my enemy. And I'm guessing he just wants to protect you."

"From what?" I demand as I take off my parka.

Ned laughs. "From older guys like me. From other people driving your car. You know."

"Someone should protect me from him."

Okay, so it was an almost-perfect day. And it's not Ned's fault that my father showed up and acted like a jerk, so I won't hold it against Ned that he wants to be civilized around the jerk. Ned can't help it if he has better manners than my father does.

I peek out the window in time to see the Explorer driving away. "I wonder why he came here in the first place," I say as I get us both a soda.

"Maybe he was just passing by."

"I doubt it. This isn't on his way to anywhere."

We finish our sodas, and Ned offers to help me set up the tree. "You have to make a fresh cut on the trunk," he tells me, "and then put it right into water."

"Are you a tree expert?"

He laughs. "No. The saw guy told me that when I took the saw back."

"There's probably a saw in the garage—that is, unless my dad has removed all his tools, although I don't know where he'd put them in his town house."

We scavenge around the garage until we find an old saw, and then I go to get the tree stand ready. Before long, we not only have the tree set up in the living room but we start decorating it too.

"Mom is going to be so happy," I tell him. "Last night she was really bummed when I didn't come home with a tree. I told her that the only ones left were too pathetic, not to mention a fire hazard, and that we might just have to go without a tree this year."

"You didn't."

"Well, I thought it would be cool to surprise her. I mean, not only is this not a dried-up old tree-lot tree but it's absolutely beautiful." I stand back and admire it.

He nods his approval. "It is a good-looking tree." Then he glances around the house. "Your place looks really Christmassy—very festive."

I laugh. "Thanks! Claire and I did most of the decorating, to help Mom out of her funk, but we used only about half of Mom's decorations. Trust me, if Mom were her usual self, this place would be *really* festive."

"Well, I think festive is fun. Your mom has the right idea."

"So have you decided what you're doing for Christmas yet, Ned?"

He just shrugs.

"Well, if you're seriously not going to Maui and you don't want to pass off that option to me, you'd be more than welcome to spend time with us. You already know my mom and most of the rest of our family. Why don't you just hang with us for the holidays?"

He brightens. "Really?"

"Yeah. We're having family and friends over on Christmas Eve, trying to act like our lives haven't totally fallen apart, and then going to Vito and Louisa's for Christmas Day. I know you'll fit right in." I laugh. "Well, other than being one of the few gringos in the mix."

"You mean I won't be the only one?" He looks disappointed.

"Sorry. Some of our other friends are gringos too, and some of our other relatives have mixed marriages. And then, of course, there's my older brother, Marc—he's bringing a gringo girl home with him."

"But I'll still be a minority?"

I nod. "Oh, yeah. I can assure you of that."

"Okay, then. I'd like to come."

I grin. "Cool."

"Well, I better split if I'm going to make it to work on time."

"Thanks for everything," I say as he leaves.

"No, thank *you.*"

"No," I tease as I wave good-bye. "Thank *you!*"

fifteen

Despite the beautiful tree and decorations, my mom is in a snit for the next couple of days. "I'm not upset with you, Maggie," she says on Saturday morning.

"Well, it sure does feel like it," I tell her as I pour a cup of coffee.

"Sorry." Lines crease her forehead. "I don't mean to take it out on you."

"Right."

"It's just so stinking unfair."

"What?"

"This." She waves her hands around as if that explains everything. I'm sure she means Dad and the big split, but this woman's mode of communication is pretty pathetic these days. I mean, she might as well start talking in Spanish, which I can understand some of and speak fairly fluently, but when she gets going fast, I am totally lost.

"What exactly?" I ask before I have to go call in an interpreter.

"Oh, finances mostly. Your father has neglected to pay a couple of bills, and I am pretty tight for money—and it's Christmas."

"Oh." I consider this. "Why don't you just use a credit card?"

She lets loose with a Spanish expletive. "Those are the bills he neglected to pay. The cards are maxed out."

"Oh." Now this is a whole new problem.

"And we've got Elisa and Marc and Liz coming, plus our little get-together on Christmas Eve." She throws her hands in the air and cuts loose with another Spanish word that she would never use in front of her mother.

"Mom," I say in a warning tone.

"Sorry."

"I get paid today," I say. "It's not much, but it might cover the party. And I've got tip money too, almost fifty dollars."

"Really? You make that much in one night?"

"No, that was for a week—well, less what I spent for the tree."

Now Mom hugs me. "Oh, *mi hija*, what would I do without you?"

I smile. "Be lonely?"

So I give Mom my tip money for groceries—enough to get us by until I get paid and hand over my check—and by the time Marc and Liz show up, she is feeling rather festive again. I, on the other hand, am feeling rather broke and slightly bummed since I had planned to go Christmas shopping for family and friends after I got paid this week.

Liz seems pretty nice, although she's kind of quiet. Marc told us she's the intellectual type—the kind of girl who likes to observe and think about things, which seems an unlikely match for my loudmouthed brother, but maybe opposites really do attract. Still, it bugs me that she stays holed up in the guest room and never offers to help in the kitchen or anything. I don't get that. And then Marc takes off to hang with his friends, and she just wants to stay here and read books or sleep.

The dynamics of our house improve greatly when Elisa gets home on Monday, just two days before Christmas. And she, amazingly, is able to draw the quiet Liz out when she proclaims it Game Night and forces the five of us to play Pictionary and Boggle until we're all totally sick of each other.

"Dad's the one who's really good at Pictionary," she tells Liz as we gather in the kitchen for a late-night snack. "His drawings were awesome."

Mom scowls darkly and then excuses herself, saying she has to work in the morning.

"What's up with her?" demands Elisa once Mom is safely upstairs.

"What do you think?" I toss back. "Be a little sensitive, would you?"

"Why?"

"Why do you think?" snaps Marc.

"She's going to have to get used to it," says Elisa. "I mean, it's a fact that couples split up all the time. And it's been like, what, three months since things really went sour? Shouldn't she be getting over it by now?"

"I don't know," I say sarcastically, "considering they were together for like twenty-five years and had three kids. She's not okay after a few months? Let's see, it took you more than a month to get over Rod, and you guys were together, like, what, six months?"

"Eight!"

"Yeah, whatever. Do the math, Elisa."

She glares at me now, and I wish I'd kept my mouth shut.

"Yeah," chimes in Marc. "Think about it, sis. Mom's still in a lot of pain. And it's Christmas. You know how lonely that would make her?"

"I do, as a matter of fact." Now she looks close to tears. "Mom's not the only one who's had her heart broken lately."

"Oh." Now I really feel bad. "Is it that guy you met at the conference?" I vaguely recall her mentioning some dude she met at a conference for her work. "Jake?"

"Jack."

"Right. So he broke up with you?"

"It was mutual."

"So that's not really the same," says Marc. "It was your choice."

"Mom had a choice in this," she says as she takes another cookie. "You can't blame it all on Dad. Divorce is always a two-way street, you know."

And suddenly we're all arguing. Oddly enough, Liz sides with Elisa. She seems certain that Mom must be somewhat to blame for the situation. How she knows this when she's barely met my family is way beyond me, but I suspect it has to do with her parents because she says they got divorced when she was six. As a result, she's an expert on the subject, which I find totally annoying. Consequently, I've decided I really don't like her much now. And considering how Marc is looking at her, I wouldn't be surprised if he feels the same way. Too bad she's going to be here all week.

I excuse myself, leaving the three of them to finish this discussion. I do feel bad for abandoning Marc and am a little worried he'll be persuaded to join the dark side before the night is over. Oh, well.

But as I get ready for bed, imagining the three of them down there bashing Mom and supporting Dad, I get really angry to think I gave up my hard-earned money just for them.

I am somewhat encouraged the next morning when I find Marc in the kitchen making coffee, and he tells me that Elisa and Liz are nuts.

"I don't get them," he says quietly as he fills the carafe with water. "How they can be so certain that Mom has a part in this—it just makes no sense."

"I wish we could all just quit talking about it," I say as I slice a piece of banana bread. "Can't we take a break from all this crud, at least during the holidays?"

"Fine by me." He turns on the coffeemaker and then looks at me. "Although I am kind of curious about his *woman*." The way he says *woman* sounds like he'd rather use a bad word but is controlling himself.

So I fill him in on what I know and have seen, glad that Mom has already gone to work. I know it would hurt her to hear this rather colorful description.

He just shakes his head. "What a jerk."

"Yeah."

"I wonder what they're doing for Christmas."

"Who cares?"

"Well, it's not like he can take her home to meet his parents."

I laugh. "Yeah, right." Dad's side of the family is even more old-fashioned than Mom's. His parents would throw a huge fit and probably disown him for good.

"Maybe they're going on a cruise," says Marc as he pours a cup of coffee.

"They better not be," I seethe.

"Why not?"

"Because Mom is broke and Dad hasn't been paying the bills."

Marc looks disgusted. "What a total jerk. I wish I could give him a piece of my mind."

"Think you can spare that much?" I tease, hoping to lighten the conversation a little.

Somehow we get through the next two days and even manage to put together a fairly decent Christmas Eve party. And when Ned shows up, I almost think it was worth giving up my paycheck to put together this little spread. Having him here makes the evening feel much merrier, and he and Marc really hit it off. In fact, we're all having a pretty good time when I suddenly notice that Mom is missing. Thinking she's in the kitchen, I go to see if she needs help with anything, but she's not there. I look downstairs, but she's not around. I glance outside to where the snow is still covering almost everything, but I don't see her out there. Finally, I go upstairs and find her in her bedroom—crying.

"Mom," I say as I enter her room without even knocking, "what's wrong?"

She just holds up her hands. "What do you think?"

I sit down on the bed next to her and put my arm around her shoulder. I don't know what to say—well, other than to curse my father for being such a moronic jerk!

"It's the . . . the first Christmas without him," she sputters in a way that almost makes it seem as if he died. I almost wish that he had—I think it would be easier. "And I just . . . just can't take it."

"I'm sorry."

"I didn't want to spoil the party," she sobs, "so I came up here."

"Want me to tell them you have a headache?" I offer.

She nods. "Yes, please do that, *mi hija*."

"All right." I pat her on the back. "And if you get to feeling better?"

"I'll come down then."

"Okay. It's really a cool party, Mom. Everyone is having a good time, and the food is great."

She almost smiles through her tears. "Good."

So I go back down and try to pretend that all is well, explaining that Mom's got a headache and will be down in a little while. No one really seems to mind, although I'm sure everyone knows what's really up. I feel somewhat relieved when Tia Louisa says she's going to check on Mom. I think she needs more comfort than I am able to give.

The party breaks up around midnight, and then Marc and Elisa help me clean up. I'm guessing Liz has sneaked off to bed, but I know better than to say anything about it.

Things start out fairly smoothly for us on Christmas Day at Vito and Louisa's. I think Mom's able to relax a bit since she's not playing hostess, and for the first hour or so, I'm impressed with how the family is being extra kind to her. I suspect that Tia Louisa has given them a private warning to be on their best behavior after Mom's little emotional breakdown last night. But as the day progresses and a couple of my uncles have had a little too much Mexican beer (and probably some tequila on the sly), things start to get out of hand. Before anyone can stop it, there is some major Roberto bashing going on, and Tio Eduardo is acting like he and "the boys" are going to drive over to Dad's place and give him "something special for Christmas."

Fortunately, the younger men (Marc and the cousins) convince the old dudes this isn't such a great idea. But it does put a damper on things. Not only that but I find it somewhat humiliating to hear the uncles bashing our "religion."

"That's what happens when people leave the church," says one of them. "They think they're better than the rest of us, and then they fall on their—"

"Shut up!" says Tia Louisa.

Fortunately, most people in our family don't question Tia Louisa. If they do, she has Tio Vito (who weighs close to three hundred pounds) to back her. But with the party starting to get out of hand, Mom decides she wants to go home. And since I'm the one who drove her here, I have to go too. I'm pretty bummed that I have to leave, since Ned is staying, and he and the cousins are having a pretty good time downstairs.

"You can stay if you like," Mom tells me as we go to the car. "I don't want to spoil your fun, Maggie. I can just drive myself home, and you can get a ride with the kids later."

I seriously consider this, but the idea of Mom sitting at home all by herself, probably crying her heart out, and on Christmas—well, that's more than I can deal with today.

"No, that's okay," I tell her. "I'm ready to go home too."

She seems satisfied with this, and the two of us drive home in silence. So much for Christmas.

Mostly I'm glad when the holidays are over. I'm relieved to go back to work on Friday. I'm also relieved when Marc and Liz leave the next day, although I would've preferred to have Marc stay a bit longer without her. I'm equally relieved when my sister leaves on Sunday.

With only a few days of Christmas break left and being nearly broke, I am totally thrilled when Ned calls and asks if I want to go sledding on Tuesday afternoon. And although I've never been sledding in my life, I accept. For one thing it's free, but besides that, it's with Ned.

He picks me up and we drive over to a hill just outside of town. "Some of my buddies are going to be there," he tells me. "I've never done this before, but they say it's pretty fun—and cheap."

"Hey, cheap works for me."

There are about a dozen college-age kids there. Someone has built a fire, and I notice there are several cases of beer. I try to act like I'm cool with this, but it still makes me uncomfortable, even more uncomfortable when I see that Ned has no problem putting away a couple.

"Aren't we going sledding?" I finally ask, hoping I don't sound too juvenile. But I feel slightly irritated that everyone here seems more interested in drinking. I can see there are several sleds (just cheap plastic ones) as well as some oversized inner tubes, and it looks like someone's been down the hill already, since there is a trail.

"You ready to hit the big slope?" teases Ned.

"Yeah," I say. "It looks like fun."

And so it seems everyone is ready to have a ride now. Ned and I watch as a couple jump on a sled and plow down the hill. Then three guys pile onto an inner tube and follow them, yipping and yelling as they go.

"Doesn't look too difficult," I say, trying to appear brave.

"Let's give it a go," says Ned. He sits down in front and I sit down in back, wrapping my arms around him.

Then down we go—and it *is* fun! We do this a couple more times, and I have to admit that I feel thirsty after climbing back up the hill, but Ned's offer of a beer doesn't tempt me much, and he doesn't push it. I've tasted beer before, one time at Tia Louisa's when I thought no one was looking. I was only thirteen then, and quite frankly I thought it tasted like something from out of a toilet. Of course, my dad found out, and he gave me a little talk and then made me promise him that I would never touch alcohol or hang with kids who did. At the time, I truly believed I would keep that promise, but now I'm not so sure—especially considering the way my dad's kept his promises lately. Maybe it just doesn't matter.

"What's your problem, Maggie?" asks one of the guys as he pops open a beer and holds it out to me in what he probably thinks is a tempting way. "Too good to have a beer with us?"

"Nope," I say suddenly, taking the beer. Why not?

He looks slightly surprised, and Ned just grins as I take a swig. It still doesn't taste too great, but I pretend I like it. And I force myself to drink the whole thing. If only Dad could see me now!

We sled some more, and I even drink a second beer. To my surprise, it doesn't taste quite as bad this time, although I'm not too crazy about the aftertaste. But with each sip, I think about how my dad would react. I imagine that this would hurt him, and that makes me feel good.

We've made lots of sled runs, and it's starting to get dusky and I am getting pretty cold. "I should probably get home," I tell Ned.

"How about one last run?"

I agree, so we get back onto the sled and Ned takes off. I can hear the crunchy sound of the ice-crusted snow as we go down the hill, and I can tell we're going lots faster than before. But I hold on tight and just pray we don't crash. We're still going fast when we reach the bottom, and instead of stopping at the mound at the end of the hill, we end up going right over it, catching air. Then *womp*—we land on top of some slushy ice that instantly turns into ice-cold water, and we are up to our waists in some kind of pond.

I'm screaming from the cold, and Ned is trying to climb out. When he finally makes it to the bank, he uses the sled to pull me out, and then we both fall down onto the bank in a freezing wet mess. But he just starts laughing, and despite my feeling a little irked, I start to laugh too. And we sit there and laugh for several minutes, but we quickly realize we need to get out of here and into dry clothes.

The others are yelling from on top of the hill, asking if we're okay, and Ned tells them that we're leaving. "And you guys might not want to take any more runs!" he yells as we walk toward his car, totally soaking wet.

"Are you sober enough to drive?" I ask as we both get in, remembering that he's had a lot more beer than I have.

"I am now," he says as he starts the engine.

And I don't argue with him because we are both shivering, and I'm pretty sure our icy plunge has sobered us both up. Soon we are at my house and, due to the fact that his heater barely works, we're both still half-frozen.

"Come in and get dry before you go home," I tell him. "You can borrow some of Marc's clothes."

So we both rush inside the house, and I show him Marc's room and the guest bathroom. "Make yourself at home," I say. "I'm sure Marc won't mind what you borrow. He's taken all the clothes he really likes to school with him."

"Are you saying I'll look like a dork?"

"A warm, dry dork," I say as I shoot into my own bathroom. I rip off my soggy clothes and take a long hot shower, running the water until my feet regain some feeling and color. I stay in there so long that I am pretty sure Ned will be gone by the time I'm done, but I don't really care. Right now I'm feeling a little irked at him—and myself too, for drinking. Or maybe I'm just irked at my dad. Whatever it is, I don't really want to see Ned right now.

Finally, I come out in my bathrobe with my hair wrapped in a towel. I hear the front door closing downstairs and figure it's Ned just leaving. Good, that way I won't have to talk to him. But when I enter the hall, I see that it's my dad just coming in.

"What are you doing here?" I demand, irritated that he thinks he can walk right into our house anytime he pleases.

He has a dark scowl on his face and is staring at the hallway behind me as if he sees something he doesn't like. "I was about to ask you the same thing, Magdela," he says in a stern tone. "And what is *he* doing here?"

I turn to see Ned just emerging from the bathroom. He's bare-chested, wearing an old pair of Marc's sweatpants and holding a T-shirt in his hand. And I suppose the two of us do look somewhat suspicious. Not that I care.

"Magdela?" my dad's voice sounds serious.

But I'm not going to take it. I turn and glare at my dad. "It's none of your business," I tell him in my most hostile voice. "You made it none of your business when you walked out of here two months ago."

"You are still my daughter."

"Not as far as I'm concerned. And if you don't leave right now, I'm going to call Mom and tell her you're here!"

For some reason, this threat works on him. I'm curious as to why he stopped by—again. Like, is he spying on my love life or something? But when he leaves, slamming the door behind him, I can tell he's really, really mad. And I can tell he thinks the worst of me and Ned, specifically that we are sleeping together. And I really don't care. In fact, I'm actually glad. It serves him right for being such a godly example in my life. Yeah, right!

sixteen

Mom is outraged when she finds out that Dad's been here. Naturally, I don't go into all the details. I just say that Ned dropped me off and Dad walked in like he owned the place. And maybe he does, legally, but only partly.

"I'm changing the locks," she announces hotly. "I'll have the locksmith come by here as soon as he's available. That should take care of it. Your father can't just walk in here whenever he likes."

"I wonder why he came over in the first place."

"Probably to take some more stuff."

"What's your lawyer say about all this?"

"Just that I'm not to sell anything. Everything will be divided up fairly when we go to court. Fifty-fifty."

I look around the house, imagining some guy with a big chain saw just sawing everything in half—half a couch, half a TV. Maybe he can just saw the house down the middle too. "How are you going to do that?" I ask. "I mean the fifty-fifty split?"

"I don't know. I might have to try to buy out your father's half of the house or make some settlement in lieu of alimony. I'm not sure."

"Oh."

"Or maybe we'll just sell the house. It's really too big for just you and me anyway, and then you'll be off to college next fall and—" Now my mom is crying again. "This is so unfair," she says between sobs. "He is ruining everything."

And it's true: He is. Or rather, he has. It's like he dropped a bomb onto our lives and leaves us to pick up the pieces, and it's so wrong.

On New Year's Eve, he drops another one. Just as I'm getting ready to go to work, trying to find a cute outfit, one that will catch Ned's eye (since I have forgiven him for the drinking/sledding day), Mom comes blasting into my room with eyes that are full of fire. She doesn't even knock.

"What is this I hear about you, Magdela?" she yells as I pull my skirt up. "You and Ned have been having sex in our house while I'm at work?"

"What?" I look at her in shock as I hurry to button my blouse. "What on earth are you talking about?"

"You and Ned, meeting here in the house for your little lovers' tryst! Right here under my own roof!"

"Mom!" I yell. "That is totally untrue. Where did you hear something so freakingly stupid anyway?"

"From your father! And that's not all. He also says you've been letting Ned drive your car. He accused me of being a neglectful parent! I want to know what is going on, and I want to know now!"

"*Nothing* is going on." I narrow my eyes as I think about how much I hate my father. "Dad is full of it! Here's the truth, Mom: Yes, I did let Ned drive my car, but only once, and that's because of the snow. You know that I have hardly ever driven on snow. We were going to get the Christmas tree, the one I bought for you because the tree lot ones were so pathetic. So when Ned told me he's driven on snow a lot for skiing and stuff, I thought we'd be safer if he drove. And as it turned out, I was right. But I swear I have never let him drive since then."

She's still scowling. "What about the other thing, Magdela. Your father said he caught you guys and that you weren't even dressed!"

"He is such a liar, Mom." So I told her what happened. "You can call Ned and ask him. In fact, he still has Marc's clothes."

"Then why did your father say that?"

I shrug. "Why does he do any of the stuff he does, Mom?" I sit down and pull on a boot. "Or maybe I know why." I look up to see her still standing there in the doorway looking totally flustered. "Maybe it's because of the way that he's living. He probably just assumes that I would drop down to his level. I swear to you, Mom, I have never had sex with Ned, or anyone, for that matter." I look right into her eyes now. "Crud, Mom, Ned has never even kissed me. For all I know, we are just friends." I just shake my head.

"Really?"

"Yeah, unfortunately."

"But you'd like to be more than friends?" She's frowning now.

"Sure, why not? But that doesn't mean I want to sleep with him, Mom. I know I'm not ready for that."

She lets loose with a Spanish swear word again, and I'm thinking this is getting way too frequent. My mom used to be so against swearing—in any language.

"Can I ask you something, Mom?" I say as I tug on the other boot.

"What?"

"Are you still a Christian?"

She stares at me like I'm losing it now. "Of course I'm still a Christian, Maggie. But you should know as well as anyone that doesn't mean I'm perfect. And with your father pushing my buttons like this, well, it's a wonder I haven't broken the law yet."

"Yet?"

She nods. "Sometimes, like right now, I feel like getting a gun and shooting that man."

I feel my brows shoot up. "Seriously?"

"Well, no, not seriously. But I wouldn't mind taking a baseball bat to his Explorer."

I stare at her, trying to determine if she's kidding.

"Oh, don't worry, I'm not going to do something stupid. But here's the honest truth: Sometimes I think I wouldn't care if my brother and his friends went over there and knocked some sense into that man, or at least encouraged the fear of God in him again."

I sort of laugh. "We're a mess, aren't we?"

"Your father's the one who's really a mess." Now she puts her face down close to mine. "And you swear that you and Ned didn't do anything disrespectful here?"

"I swear."

And she curses again in Spanish. Then she marches out of the room, and the next thing I hear is her yelling into the phone, also in Spanish, and she's talking so fast that I can't understand most of it, except that she's talking to my dad and she is furious.

Mama mia! Sometimes I wonder about my mother.

As I drive to the restaurant, I hope Mom gets her anger under control by the time I get home. And then it occurs to me, oh yeah, this is New Year's Eve, the one night of the year when my parents always went out. I remember when I was little, I would be so awed by how Mom would get all dressed up, just like a movie star.

Sometimes I would sit in the bedroom and watch her adding the final touches to her hair and jewelry and makeup. She still had her jet-black hair and sparkling eyes. I thought she was so amazingly beautiful. And I guess she still is—in a softer, rounder, more faded sort of way. Still, I realize now how she won't be getting all dressed up tonight, how she will probably be sitting home and thinking about what used to be and feeling depressed as a result.

I mention my concerns to Tia Louisa before the restaurant gets busy. "Do you think she'd want to come here?" I ask. "Maybe just to hang out?"

Tia Louisa frowns. "I don't know why, Magdela. We're going to be very busy tonight. Unless Rosa wants to help out, which I seriously doubt, she would probably be bored stiff."

"Oh."

"But call her if you like. It's worth a shot, eh?"

So I quickly call home, and to my surprise, she doesn't answer. Then, feeling seriously worried for her welfare and her depressed mental state (not to mention some of her comments about my dad), I decide to try her cell phone. To my relief, she picks up.

"Oh, don't worry about me, Maggie," she assures me. "I'm just meeting some friends from work tonight. We're going to have a little celebration of our own for New Year's."

"You're sure you'll be okay?"

She laughs. "Yes, dear. But I do appreciate your concern. And drive carefully on your way home. There will be lots of kooks on the road tonight."

"Okay, you too. And don't drink and drive, Mom. You know you can always call me if you need a ride."

"Yes, dear," she says in a slightly irritated tone. "I will keep that in mind."

As I hang up, I think about how funny it is that I'm starting to act more and more like the parent.

The restaurant is very busy. I work later than usual, until ten thirty, seating the last people to come in. I stick around for a while after my shift just helping out and hoping to get a quick visit with Ned, but everyone is busy with the lively crowd, and eventually I realize that I'm pretty tired so I decide to go home.

And here's what's ironic: I'm the one sitting at home by herself, ringing in the New Year with a bowl of ice cream and the TV as the big ball in Times Square gets lowered at the stroke of midnight. Happy New Year. You bet.

I'm sort of glad to get back to the routine of classes when Christmas break ends. I'm also glad to see Claire again, although her tan is making me seriously jealous.

"Oh, you should talk, Maggie," she says to me after I comment on it for like the tenth time. "You're the one who gets to look tan year-round."

"Yeah, right. I think I'm about the color of cornmeal right now."

"Do a tanning bed," she suggests.

"Yeah, like Mom will let me do that."

"Well, at least you got to do some fun things with Ned," she tosses back at me.

I smile and nod. I told her about getting the tree and the Christmas parties and even sledding and getting dunked in the pond. Okay, I didn't include all the details. She would frown on the idea of me hanging out with college kids who were drinking. And I suppose I might've made some things sound better than they actually were. But, hey, a girl's got to have something.

Especially when her family seems to be racing downhill. First my mom threw a fit when my dad called her an unfit mother. Then my dad threw a fit when Mom changed the locks. And since then, it's been back and forth. It seems like they're arguing as much now as when he was living at home, except now it's way more hateful. Of course, I only hear Mom's end on the phone, but I can tell by the long, angry pauses that he's getting in his shots. And instead of getting better or getting over this, Mom seems to be getting more and more bitter.

She also seems to be changing. I'm not sure when it first started. Maybe it was New Year's Eve, or maybe it was even sooner; I just wasn't paying attention. All I know is that two weeks have passed since New Year's, and Mom is way different.

First she got her hair cut and colored to cover the gray. And to be honest, even though it was kind of shocking to see her in short hair, it really does look better. And she looks younger too. I think she's done something with her makeup. Then she decided to join a fitness club. Not a bad idea either, although I think she might be spending too much time there. Plus, she's started lecturing me about why I should exercise. And then she starts this low-carb diet where she eats mostly eggs and meat and dairy products. I'm not even sure how it works, but she seems to think it does.

Now, all this isn't such a problem, except that she's kind of obsessed over it and can get kind of preachy. She's acting like she's always been some kind of health freak, which is totally not true. But what worries me even more is that she's been starting to buy stuff.

"How can you afford that?" I ask when I see her sporting a new workout outfit that looks expensive.

"How could I not afford it?" she tosses back at me like she's forty-five going on fifteen. "Don't I look awesome in it?"

Awesome? Since when does my mom use that word? "But how did you pay for it?" I persist like I'm seventeen going on fifty. "I thought we were kind of broke."

She grins. "I opened a new account at Nordstrom's."

"Oh."

"Don't worry. I've got a sale pending on a really good house. I'll pay off the card as soon as it closes."

"Right."

"Until then, you can't blame me for getting a few things. I've already dropped one dress size." She turns around showing off her figure, which I can't deny does look better.

But here's the weirdest part: As she's doing this little look-at-me routine, she reminds me of someone. And I study her for a few seconds, taking in her pale-pink velour sweats, and it hits me that she reminds me of Stephanie, my dad's girlfriend! And I'm thinking this cannot be. And I also notice she looks a lot tanner than usual too.

"Have you been going to a tanning salon?" I ask her in an accusatory tone.

She gives me a sly grin. "Shawna at work talked me into it. What do you think, Maggie?" She actually pulls up her top to expose her wrinkly brown tummy, and I'm thinking, *Ee-uuw, gimme a break.* But I know better than to say it. Despite Mom's bravado, she's still fragile underneath.

"But I thought you said tanning beds were dangerous, Mom."

She shrugs. "They might be. You should see all the warnings they post in there, Maggie. If you read them, you'd understand why I'm concerned."

"But you go anyway?"

"The way I see it, it's better than smoking."

"Smoking?" Now I'm seriously confused. My mom has never smoked in her life.

"Yeah, I was thinking of taking it up."

"No way!"

She laughs. "Yeah, I decided to try tanning instead."

"Oh, man." I just shake my head as I fish in my purse for my keys. "I better go or I'll be late for work."

"Lighten up, Maggie," she says playfully.

I look up and study her face. "Lighten up?"

"Yeah. Life's too short to be mad all the time."

"So you're not mad at Dad anymore?" I ask in disbelief.

Now she gets a very sour expression. "I never said that."

"What then?"

"I'm just trying to focus on me for a change."

"Does that help?"

"It helps me block out your father."

"So you're not bitter anymore?"

"Only when I think about him."

Why does it feel like we're never going to get over this? I think about my mom's last comment as I drive to work. It's like she's stuck—like no matter how hard she tries, she can't get away from the pain. I just don't get why Dad's big mistake continues to hang over our heads like this nasty, dark cloud, yet he just gets to go on his merry little way as if nothing's wrong.

seventeen

"You're too young for me," Ned teases me as we stand in the parking lot after work on Friday night after our shift ends. Okay, I've been shamelessly flirting with him all night, trying to get him to look at me as something beyond his "little friend" or younger sister. But it's like I just can't get this guy to take me seriously. I think it might have something to do with the fact that he turned twenty-one just a week ago, and now it's like suddenly he's oh so much older and far more sophisticated than me. It's totally unfair.

"I like older men," I tell him in my most seductive voice.

He laughs. "Probably just a daddy complex."

I sock him in the arm. "Get real!" But I'm surprised that his accusation hits closer to home than I care to admit. I actually wonder if my fixation on Ned might be a result of feeling abandoned by my dad or if I'm just trying to get back at Dad and make him sorry for being such a cruddy excuse for a father. Or maybe I'm just making something out of nothing.

"You're just a baby, Maggie," he says, not so teasing this time. "Go get a boy your own age."

"I'll be eighteen in less than a month," I remind him in a sharp tone. "That's old enough to legally vote and buy cigarettes."

153

"Impressive."

"Fine, whatever!" I snap as I turn to go to my car. Why do I even bother with this guy?

"Wait," he says, grabbing my hand and pulling me over to him.

I barely breathe as he puts his face close to mine, staring at me under the parking lot lights. "Why?" I ask, hoping to seem difficult now, like he's the one chasing me, not the other way around.

"You really think you're ready for this?"

"For what?" I say defiantly.

Then he leans down and kisses me, long and hard. And I kiss him back with equal passion. And as we're kissing, I'm thinking, *This is so right. This is so good. This is what I've been waiting for.* I assure myself that it has nothing to do with my stupid dad or my parents' unfortunate problems. This is my life, and I'll live it how I want!

And I feel like I'm truly grown-up now, like I'm in control of my own life, and it's like I can hear wedding bells and see us walking down the aisle together—officially Mr. and Mrs. Ned Schlamowski, off to live happily ever after.

Finally, he stops kissing me, and then he steps away, looking over his shoulder nervously. "Man, I hope your aunt's not watching."

"It's okay," I assure him, although I seriously hope the same thing.

"I've got to go," he says as he reaches into his pocket for his keys.

"Why?" I ask. "Where are you going?"

"I promised to meet some friends."

I make a frown. "So that's it then? Just kiss me and drive away?"

"What do you want, Maggie?"

Now I start to pout. "Fine. Whatever." And I walk away, feeling like I've been slapped.

"Look," he says as he follows me to my car. "I'd invite you to come with me, but we're meeting at a bar. It's not like you can get in, you know." Then he looks hopeful. "Unless you have a fake ID. You don't, do you?"

I just shake my head.

"I didn't think so. Besides, it's a bad idea. Louisa would have a fit if she knew I took you to a bar."

"Why don't you tell your friends you're busy?" I suggest. "Then we could do something."

"Like what?" He pulls me over to him now, holding me close again. "What would you suggest we do?"

"I don't know," I say breathlessly.

He leans down and kisses me again and then suddenly stops. "We can't keep doing this out here, Maggie. It's an accident waiting to happen."

"Let's go someplace," I suggest, feeling reckless. "Meet somewhere."

He runs his hand through his hair. "Where?"

"Your place?"

Now he laughs. "Yeah, right. My roommates would really like that."

"Oh."

We see the back door to the restaurant open, and now Susan is walking toward us and I am feeling desperate. "Come to my house," I say quietly. "My mom is out tonight."

He nods and we say good night as if we're not planning on meeting again. Then we get in our cars and I drive home as fast as

I can, hoping that Mom is still out with her friends, which is likely since this is Friday and she's been staying out later and later.

I get to my house before Ned and quickly run into the house to make sure she's not home, and she's not. Then I go outside to wait for Ned. When he arrives, I ask him to park his car down the street and around the corner.

"Just in case my mom gets home," I say.

He laughs at me but agrees, and soon we are sitting on the couch together. I'm drinking a soda and I have actually let him have one of the Corona beers my mom has been stocking in the fridge lately "for friends," and I figure that should include Ned.

Before long, we are kissing again, and I can tell Ned's experienced at this—way more so than any of the high school guys I've gone out with, and way more than me. And soon I realize he's expecting more—more than I have ever given, more than I ever intended on giving, at least until my wedding day. I know he's expecting what Tia Dominga calls "the whole enchilada," and we all know what she means by that. And a part of me wants to do this. A part of me wants to play the grown-up and even throw this all back in my dad's face just to show him. But another part is unsure that I'm ready for the next step.

Finally, I pull away with some seriously cold feet. "I can't do this," I say, trying to catch my breath.

He frowns and just shakes his head. "I knew this would happen, Maggie. You lead a guy on like this when you're really just a little girl."

"I'm just not ready," I say, standing up and smoothing my clothes back into place.

He stands up too. "Yeah, that's what I'm saying. You're too young. Don't you get it?" He looks mad now, and for a moment I consider giving in—like it's the only way to get this guy, the only way to hold on to him. Isn't that what all guys (including my dad) are looking for? Why not just give in? But then I imagine my mom walking in, and the idea of her finding us doing it is way too scary.

"You're just pushing me too fast," I tell him. "I need time."

"Yeah, like a few more years. Call me when you're grown-up, Maggie." Then he picks up his coat and walks out. And now I'm angry, and not just at him either. I'm angry at myself, at my life, at my parents—everything.

"What *is* holding you back?" I ask myself as I stomp up the stairs. It's not like anyone in my family would really care, would they? I mean, my mom might be mad for a while, but then she's so checked out she'd probably forget all about it in a day or two. And my dad—well, who gives a flying fig about what he thinks anyway? Besides, this is a good way to get even. And then I consider how everyone and everything is forcing me to act like a grown-up anyway. My days of being a kid are over. Why not go all the way? "Just grow up, Maggie!" I yell as I slam the door to my room.

But on Saturday, the day after my failed attempt to get Ned to take me seriously, I decide that it's time to take the next step. Today is the day. Tonight will be the night. I am ready for this. I am grown-up.

I spend the morning getting the perfect outfit ready, clear down to the undies, which are lacy and so hot. Then I shower and shampoo and condition my hair and very carefully shave my legs. I even take a nap. I want to be so ready for this. I am not going to blow it tonight.

I have it all planned out. I'll ask Tia Louisa to cash my check, and then I will tell Ned I'll pay for a hotel room with my own money. How can Ned argue with that? I've already written Mom a note telling her that I'm spending the night with Claire. Knowing Mom, she will not call to check on me. She never has. And even if she did, she would probably try my cell phone first. And I will leave it turned on, just in case.

Okay, I feel really nervous as I drive to work. But I tell myself I can do this. I am a grown-up, I have my own job, my own car, and I pretty much have to pay for everything myself these days—not to mention contribute to the household expenses. What about this is not grown-up?

Once again, I flirt with Ned. But he is indifferent, like he's still irked about last night. But then he doesn't know yet what I have planned for tonight. I am waiting to surprise him out in the parking lot. I can't wait to see his face when he hears my plans. Finally, my shift comes to an end and the restaurant is surprisingly quiet for a Saturday night, but I think that has to do with the weather, which is icy and cold and miserable.

"I need to talk to you," I whisper to Ned as he puts away the dessert tray. "After work tonight, okay?"

He just nods as he sets the tray back into place. Then I make a quick run to the restroom, check my hair, reapply lip gloss, and critique my appearance in the mirror. My hair is up and my mom's diamond stud earrings (I figure she shouldn't mind since she's been borrowing my stuff) look very sophisticated. I so want to look perfect for Ned. Then I go to Tia Louisa's office to pick up my check.

"Would you mind cashing it for me?" I ask hopefully.

She peers up at me over her reading glasses, studying me for a few seconds. "What's the occasion?"

"I told Mom I could give her some grocery money," I say quickly. And I'm surprised to find that I actually feel guilty about this particular lie, mostly because Tia Louisa has been so good to me. On the other hand, I have absolutely no desire to tell her what I actually plan to do with the money tonight either. That would be suicidal. "And since we weren't too busy tonight"—at least this part's true—"tips were a little thin."

"You're a good girl to help your mom like this, Magdela," she says as she takes my signed check, unlocks a drawer, and then counts out some cash.

"Thanks." I take the cash and decide that I'll have to make good on this by actually giving Mom some grocery money tomorrow—when I get home, that is.

"Drive carefully," she warns me. "It's slick out there."

"I will," I promise.

Then, feeling a mixture of nerves and excitement, I go out to the restaurant and see that some of the waiters have already left—including Ned. I figure he's probably in the parking lot since I told him I needed to talk, so I get my coat and purse and, holding my head high, go out to tell him my plan.

But I don't see him in the icy parking lot, and when I look around, I see that his car is gone, and I realize that he left—just blew me off, just like that—and I am furious.

I get into my car, turning the engine on and hoping to get warm. I sit there and wait, just in case he comes back. But after a few minutes, I realize this is pretty stupid, so I decide to drive around a little to see if I can spot his bug somewhere. But after half an hour, I realize that I'm just wasting gas, so I go home.

I'm relieved to find that Mom's not home. I suspect she already read my note and is just assuming I'm at Claire's. She's probably using me as an excuse to stay out even later than usual tonight, just hanging with her friends and having a good time. Unlike me, she's having a life.

But here's what's weird: As I get ready for bed, I have this sense of relief way down inside of me. Even though I still feel irked at Ned, I'm thinking I really wasn't ready to have sex. And having sex probably wouldn't have made me any more grown-up than remaining a virgin. If anything, it probably would've really complicated my life. And the fact that a part of me would be doing it for revenge—to get back at my dad and to hurt him—is kind of freaky. Like sacrificing a part of myself would make things better? Something's wrong with my thinking.

eighteen

Now, it's not that I blame Mom for wanting to change herself and have a life, but I'm starting to find it kind of unsettling. I've not only lost a dad but I could be losing my mom as well. Okay, maybe I'm overreacting, but she really does seem changed to me, like she thinks she's suddenly turned into my sister or something. To be honest, I thought maybe she was just going through a phase at first, I mean with her fitness kick, new haircut, and stuff. I figured she'd get tired of trying so hard and go back to her old mom-like self. But a month has gone by, and she seems to only be getting worse. Not only is she borrowing my clothes but she almost looks better in them than I do—and if you ask me, that's pretty disturbing.

"Your mom sure looks hot today," Claire notices when she picks me up for school. "Hey, are those your Nine West boots?"

I nod and climb into her car. "She thinks she's like eighteen now."

Claire laughs. "Speaking of eighteen, I know someone who has a birthday this week."

"That's right." I slap myself on the forehead. "I almost forgot." The truth is, I've been depressed lately. The whole thing with Ned has really gone south on me, and it's like every day is just one big drag.

"So are you getting the night off on Saturday?"

"I forgot to ask."

"Maggie! You have to get it off—it's your birthday and we need to celebrate. Youth group is planning a surprise for you."

"Youth group?" I consider this. It seems like years since I've been to youth group.

"Yeah, remember youth group?" she asks with sarcasm. "You used to go there every Saturday night with me."

"I know, but Saturday is a busy night for the restaurant."

"I'm sure your aunt will give you the night off for your birthday. She can't be that mean."

"She's not mean."

"I thought you said she was."

"I used to think that, back when I was a little kid. But that's just because she's very direct and never puts up with crud—not from anyone."

"So why don't you be direct with her and ask for the night off."

So I tell Claire that I will, but when I get the chance to ask Tia Louisa later that night, I don't. Don't ask me why—I just don't. Maybe I'm hoping that something with Ned will change, like maybe he'll find out it's my birthday and do something special for me on Saturday, kind of like the night of the Harvest Dance. That was so sweet. Or maybe I don't ask her simply because I don't want to go to youth group and any excuse is a good excuse. I'm probably worried that my old youth-group friends will see right through me and realize I'm not exactly living the Christian life anymore. It's not like I'm out there sinning big-time, although I probably would if I could, but I guess I've pretty much let my faith go sideways. Of course, I think my dad is mostly to blame for this lack of spiritual interest, and not just for me either. My whole family seems a little lost right now.

On Friday, Claire asks me about my birthday again, and I actually lie to her this time. "My aunt can't get anyone to work for me," I tell her, acting like I'm really disappointed.

"No way."

I nod. "Bummer, huh?"

"You really have to work on your eighteenth birthday?"

"It's okay," I assure her. "We can really use the money. My dad has totally flaked on us, and my mom hasn't sold anything all month."

Naturally, I don't tell her my theory behind Mom's lack of sales—that she hasn't been trying too hard or that she spends more time at the fitness center than at the office. And no way do I tell Claire about Rich, the guy Mom's been starting to hang out with. Mostly I'm hoping that Rich is just a temporary lapse in good judgment. But when I come home from work on Friday night, Rich's car (a hideous black El Camino that's been restored to within an inch of its life) is parked out front.

So I enter the house through the garage and tiptoe through the dark kitchen, hoping I can slip upstairs without actually seeing him—or them. I hear what sounds like some lame disco music coming from the living room and I think I'm clear to go, but no such luck.

"Is that you, Maggie?" my mom calls just as I reach the foot of the stairs.

"Yeah, I'm just going to bed."

"Come in and say hello first."

So I go over and tip my head into the room and offer an unenthusiastic hello.

"Hey, Maggie," says Rich from where he's sitting on the couch, wearing a shiny black shirt that's open at the neck and showing off way too much gold jewelry. With his slicked-back hair and cocky smile, this guy is like a bad cliché for Latinos. I cannot imagine what Tia Louisa would say if she ever met him. I just hope she never does.

"How was work?" my mom asks. I notice that she's wearing my favorite skirt and that it's riding up pretty high, revealing more thigh than I'd be comfortable with. Can't she even see that?

"Busy," I say, turning away. "Good night."

"Night, Maggie," my mom calls sweetly after me.

"Don't let the bed bugs bite," calls Rich.

I roll my eyes and suppress the urge to scream *ee-uuw!* as I head up the stairs. I go to my room and close the door and realize that I hate my life. I really do. I hate my dad, I hate who my mom is becoming, I definitely hate Rich, and I even hate Elisa and Marc right now—first of all because they are so far away and removed from all this stupidity, and second of all because they don't even seem to care. I also hate school and all my boring friends. I hate the weather—cold and gloomy. I hate my job and the way everyone there seems to take me for granted. And I hate Ned.

Okay, maybe I don't actually hate Ned, but I'm really mad at him. It's like he's not even giving me the time of day lately. And Susan said that she thinks he has a girlfriend. A girlfriend! Not only that but I noticed he changed the schedule and won't even be working tomorrow night. Man, I so hate my life.

I sleep in late on Saturday, and when I get up, I'm still in a real snit. I go downstairs to see that Mom hasn't gotten up yet, or if she did, she didn't clean up a single thing from her and Rich's little party last night. The sight of our living room littered with beer bottles, leftover pizza, paper plates, and crud just makes me want to throw something. Our place never used to look like this. There used to be order and neatness and a sense that life had some kind of meaning. Now it just feels hopeless, pathetic, and random. I hate it. And I am not cleaning this up.

I get a bowl of cereal and go back to my room and wish I had someplace to go today. I wish I had some money so I could at least go to the mall and pretend to have a life.

"This is all your freaking fault, Dad!" I scream as I actually throw my cereal bowl against my door, leaving a ding in the wood and a mess of soggy cornflakes, milk, and broken glass all over the carpet. Then I throw myself across my bed and just cry. You'd think my tears would help alleviate my rage, but it's like I'm just getting madder and madder. I even consider going over to Dad's stupid town house and throwing a complete fit. Or maybe, like Mom considered doing once, I could take my brother's baseball bat to Dad's Explorer and beat the bloody chrome off of it.

Instead, I just eat and sleep all day. Hey, it's my birthday. I deserve to pig out on junk food and possibly put on a pound or two. Who cares? Finally, it's time to get ready for work, and I consider calling in sick but just can't bring myself to do that to Tia Louisa. Despite my misery, I still care what she thinks of me. Besides, she's been having some awful migraines lately, and I don't want to add to her stress.

"Happy birthday," I tell myself as I drive to work. Okay, I'm not a bit surprised that Dad totally forgot my birthday. I mean, I never expected him to remember—didn't even want him to. But I do feel hurt that Mom didn't do anything or even say anything—not that I really thought she would, as consumed as she is with her own life and stupid Rich right now. And, okay, maybe I am enjoying this little pity party a little too much. Why shouldn't I?

Work is a drag. I mean, it's busy and the time goes by pretty quickly, but working on your birthday is so wrong. As I pick up my check and tell my aunt good night, I am on the verge of tears.

"Are you okay, Magdela?" she asks with a frown.

"Just bummed."

She nods. "Any particular reason?"

I can tell by her expression that her head is probably hurting, so I decide not to burden her with my troubles. It's not like she can do anything about them anyway. "Just life."

She kind of smiles. "Yes, I know how that can be."

"So what do you do about it?" I ask suddenly. "I mean, how do you deal with it without losing your mind?"

She looks slightly surprised. "I would think you'd know the answer to that one, Magdela."

"Why?"

"Well, I guess because of things that Rosa has told me in the past."

"Huh?"

She gives me that look—the one she uses to correct my bad grammar or warn me to mind my manners.

"I mean, *pardon?*"

She nods, satisfied. "Well, a few years ago, your mother gave me quite a little speech about praying and how there are ways to pray your own prayers without using a rosary—prayers that come right from your heart."

I study her for a long moment. "So do you do that? Do you pray right from your heart?"

"Sometimes." She sighs. "Like when I'm having an especially bad headache, or when I'm worried about my boys."

I'm sure my face looks surprised or maybe even skeptical.

"I suppose I thought you did the same, Magdela."

I think about this. "I used to."

"Used to?"

Now I'm uncomfortable. I can't believe that Tia Louisa is actually talking to me about praying. My parents always acted like the rest of their family, the ones who go to the traditional Catholic church, were somehow less spiritual than our family, as if they didn't have a personal relationship with God or were somehow less "born again." Once again, it looks like we were wrong.

"Maybe you should try it again," she tells me with a half smile. "I don't think it could hurt."

I nod, swallowing against the lump in my throat.

"Don't forget your paycheck," she says, nodding to the table where, as usual, they are laid out.

"Thanks," I tell her, picking it up. "You know what?" I say suddenly, not even sure why, except maybe I just need some sympathy.

"What, Magdela?"

"It's my eighteenth birthday today." And then I start crying. "And no one even remembered."

She gets up from her chair now, comes over, and puts her arms around me. "Oh, Magdela, I'm so sorry. I completely forgot."

"No, that's okay, Tia Louisa. But Mom forgot too. And, of course, Dad did. And I don't know why, but it really hurts. It's like my family is gone—like they've been nuked or something. I just hate it."

She strokes my hair now. "Poor Maggie. It's been a hard year for you."

I consider telling her about Ned too but think better of it. Finally, I quit crying, and she hands me a tissue. "Thanks for letting me dump on you."

"Glad I could be here. And believe it or not, Maggie, this too will pass. And in the end, you really will be stronger for it. Trust me, you will." She looks thoughtful as she strokes the silver crucifix hanging so elegantly over her black cashmere sweater.

I nod. "I hope so."

"In the meantime, you might want to try praying again."

"Yeah, you're probably right."

"Happy birthday."

"Thanks."

Then she unlatches her crucifix and hands it to me. "This is for you, Magdela."

I feel my eyes opening wide as I stare at the beautiful piece of jewelry. I know it's been in the family for generations. In fact, my mom has often wished it were hers. "No way. You can't be serious."

"I am serious. Happy birthday."

"But—"

"Please don't argue with me, Magdela. That piece was given to me by my father, your grandfather. It was his mother's and her mother's before her, and so on. I have the history all written out at home. Because Papa had no sisters and he was the oldest son, it was given to him, and he saved it for his firstborn daughter, which was me. And now, as you know, I have no daughters."

"But what about a granddaughter someday?"

She laughs. "Knowing my two boys, well, I'm not holding my breath." Then she puts her hand on my shoulder. "If I'd had a daughter, Magdela, I would've wanted her to be just like you."

I don't know what to say, and I feel fresh tears coming, but these are a different kind of tears.

As I drive home, I think about what Tia Louisa said about praying. Who would've thought she had a real relationship with God? I mean, it's not that she ever seemed like a bad person, but she's never really talked about her faith much before—maybe because my parents were always talking about theirs so much, trying to convince everyone in the family to come to our reformed church. Not that there's anything wrong with our church. I know there's not. I guess there was just something wrong with us—or Dad, since he sort of started this whole mess.

Mom's not home when I get there. I assume she's out with stupid Rich again, and I don't know if I even care anymore. It's not like I can do anything about it anyway. I feel exhausted as I get ready for bed, like I could sleep for a week. But before I go to sleep, I remember my aunt's encouragement and actually manage to eke out a pathetic little prayer.

"God, help me," I whisper into the darkness. "I know that I need to talk to you, but I'm not sure what I should say. It's been so long. I'm not even sure you'll want to talk to me at all. Please help me out of this dark hole."

The next morning, I am surprised to wake up fairly early— early enough to go to church, although I tell myself that I don't have to go, that no one will miss me or care whether I show or not. After all, I haven't been there in weeks. Plus, as quiet as the house is, I'm pretty sure Mom will be sleeping in today. I am positive she has no plans to go to church. We don't even talk about it anymore. It's like that part of our lives, like so much else, is just over now.

But then, just as I'm taking a swig of orange juice, I realize that I *want* to go to church. I really do want to go. I glance up at the kitchen clock and see that I can still make it if I hurry, so I hurry. I throw on the same outfit I wore to work last night and hop in my car and go.

I walk into the service just as the worship music begins, and as I slip into one of the back rows, it feels so right. The music sounds so good, so familiar, and I realize that I feel more at home here than I have felt anywhere during these last few months. Then Father Thomas begins to speak, and the words of his sermon slice right through the thick of my life, cutting me right where it hurts—where it hurts so good—and there are tears running down my face.

nineteen

As I'm driving home from church pondering Father Thomas's words, my cell phone begins to chime. Since I'm not in traffic I decide to answer, but when I hear Mom's slightly hysterical voice I pull over.

"What is it?" I ask her with mild irritation. She's turned into the drama queen of the family, a role that used to be designated to me.

"It's Louisa," she sobs.

"Tia Louisa?" I ask.

"Yes. She . . . she's dead, Maggie."

I feel everything around me start to shake as if I'm experiencing an earthquake, but then I realize it's just me. "Mom?" I say loudly, certain that I've gotten this wrong somehow. "Did I hear you right? What did you just say?"

"Louisa is dead. She got one of her migraines early this morning and—and it got worse and she passed out and Vito called 911 and they think she had an aneurism or a blood clot, but she died instantly." She lets out a loud cry. "My only sister is dead!"

"I'm almost home, Mom," I tell her as I start driving again. My hands are shaking so hard that I'm not sure I can actually steer, and the tears blurring my eyes make it hard to see, but somehow I get there within minutes. I run into the house and find Mom still in her bathrobe and just sobbing. I hug her, and we hold on to each other for several minutes just crying hard.

"I really loved Tia Louisa," I say to Mom when we finally quit hugging and sit down. "I cannot believe she's gone." Then I remember her gift to me last night. I hold it up for Mom to see.

"Louisa's crucifix!" she shrieks as if I had stolen it. "Where did you get it?"

"She gave it to me last night," I explain. "For my birthday."

Mom's eyes grow wide. "Your birthday, *mi hija*, oh, dear! I totally forgot."

"I know."

"And Louisa gave you this?" She reaches to touch the cross, almost as if it is holy. "I can't believe it."

"I couldn't believe it either, Mom, but she insisted." Then I tell her the whole story, including what my aunt said about praying.

My mom looks incredulous. "Louisa really said that?"

"She did. And because of her, I did pray again. It was the first time in months, Mom. And then I even went to church today, all because of her." Now I start crying again. "I can't believe she's really gone. I am going to miss her so much."

The extended family gathers at Vito and Louisa's house in the afternoon. I guess it's kind of like a wake. The women cook lots of food and cry. The men stay in the living room drinking and crying too. Everyone is talking about Louisa, remembering things, saying how she will be missed and what a fine woman she was. By evening, her sons have made it into town, and there is more food and more crying. Finally, the group begins breaking up, until Mom and I are the only ones left except for Louisa's immediate family.

Vito looks at the crucifix hanging around my neck. "Louisa told me about that," he says. "That she gave it to you for your birthday last night. She seemed happy about doing that." And then he starts crying again and I hug him.

"Tia Louisa was amazing," I say quietly. "I will never, never forget her, Tio Vito, not for as long as I live." I stop hugging him and then tap my chest. "She is going to be with me in here—always."

He nods sadly, thanks me, and then turns away.

Mom and I are silent as I drive us home. It's like there are no more words to say—just sadness, and missing.

Tia Louisa's funeral is held at Saint Peter's downtown on Thursday. I haven't been to this church since my grandfather died almost two years ago, but I am once again astounded at the old-world beauty of the carvings and windows and artwork. I am also astounded at the nerve of my father to show his face at her funeral. And it's no surprise that no one speaks to him. He is properly shunned. But I must admit to feeling just a little bit sorry for him as I see him slinking out a side door afterward. He looks like a beaten man to me, and I wonder whether his wonderful new life has really been as great as he expected it would be.

After the service, there is a reception at the restaurant, which will be closed until next week. Tio Eduardo is handling all the restaurant details, as well as the reception today. He's had the whole thing catered and made sure that all the restaurant staff was invited. And now it seems quite natural that they're mixing with all of Louisa's relatives and expressing their sympathy to poor Tio Vito, whose eyes are bloodshot from too many tears and, according to my mom, too much tequila.

"I'm sorry," Ned says when I finally run into him on my way to the ladies' room. "For your loss, I mean."

I nod somberly. "Thanks."

"She was a great woman."

"Yes, she was."

"And I'm sorry about us too," he says quietly. "I know I hurt you, Maggie, and I never meant to—not really."

"It's okay," I tell him. And strangely enough, as I walk away, I think it actually is okay. Whether it's the shock of losing my aunt or the fact that I know I am returning to my faith once again, I realize that I am really over him. I have absolutely no desire to be involved with him, none at all—well, other than as coworkers. And since I promised Tio Eduardo that I would continue working in the restaurant, I can see that it's inevitable—and probably for the best too.

"It's what Tia Louisa would expect me to do," I told my uncle earlier this week when he was trying to decide whether to reopen or to shut the place down for good.

He nodded. "Yes, I'm sure you're right. And I'm sure she would want Casa del Sol to go on as well."

Both Elisa and Marc made it here for the funeral, and after the reception, the four of us drive home together in Mom's car—almost like old times, except, of course, Dad is missing.

"I can't believe that Dad had the nerve to show up today," says Marc bitterly. "He obviously has no respect for the dead."

I consider this, wondering what Tia Louisa would really think about my dad's appearance at her funeral. I think back to the times when she and I talked about him in regard to my parents' marriage breakup. She was surprisingly gracious. In fact, she even told me that I should listen to his side of the story too and also that I should never forget that he is still my father.

As Mom and Marc, and now even Elisa, do a thorough job of Dad bashing, I am starting to recall the sermon that hit me so hard last Sunday, shortly before I learned of my aunt's death. It was about forgiveness, and it actually sounded somewhat familiar. In fact, I think Father Thomas preached about this exact same thing last fall, when I pretty much ignored his words. Perhaps I wasn't the only one. Maybe Father Thomas realizes we need to hear about this particular topic on a fairly regular basis. I'm sure that I do since I obviously didn't get it then. Maybe I don't even totally grasp it now.

But as I hear Marc going on and on about Dad and how messed up he is and how he hopes Mom's divorce lawyer really takes him to the cleaners later this month, I realize with a very distinct clarity that I need to forgive my dad. But even as this hits me, I have no idea how I can accomplish such a feat, and so I silently pray, asking God to help me.

After we get home, I hang out with my family for a while, but it's not long before they're all doing their own thing. Marc is watching a basketball game, Elisa is doing something on the computer, and Mom is going over some paperwork for a house she thinks may have sold.

Without telling anyone where I'm going, I slip out, get in my car, and start driving toward Dad's place. This time, unlike the last time, I pull over and call him first. No way do I want to interrupt anything with Stephanie.

"Yes, I am home, Maggie," he says, sounding eager. "Do you want to stop by?"

"Yes," I say, hoping that I can do this—that I won't chicken out. "See you in a few minutes."

And the next thing I know, I am there, walking toward the town house and wishing I'd thought to ask him to meet me someplace else. "Dear God, help me," I whisper as I go up the stairs. But then I notice that his Explorer isn't parked in his space, and I wonder if perhaps he's the one who chickened out and left. But when I knock on the door, he opens it and gives me a sad little smile.

"It's been a while," he says as he opens the door.

I notice right away that he's shaved his stupid goatee, but he appears to have several days of stubble on his face, and his hair has grown out to how it used to be, except that it looks uncombed and dirty. "Yeah, it has," I say as I go inside.

Not much seems to have changed in his town house—well, other than it's a lot messier than before. Newspapers and dishes and clutter seem to be all over the place, and it smells pretty stale, kind of like gross laundry that's been sitting too long. He clears off a spot for me to sit, and I just shake my head. "Can't say much for your housekeeping, Dad."

He looks embarrassed. "Sorry."

"Doesn't Stephanie know how to clean?"

"Oh, we broke up."

"Really?" I study him more closely now. My observations from the funeral seem to be spot-on. He does look like a beaten man. "What happened?"

He looks unsure as to whether he wants to tell me.

"Come on," I urge him. "What happened?"

So then he just opens up, pouring out the saddest story of how the boss found out that he and Stephanie were "involved" and how that was strictly against corporate policy.

I just shake my head, but I guess I'm thinking he was asking for it.

"He called Stephanie in to talk to him first," Dad continues. "I didn't even know about it. And she, well, she was really worried about losing her job. She's got a little boy, you know."

"I didn't know."

"Well, yeah, she does. And she didn't want to get fired, so she told the boss that I had sexually harassed her."

I feel my eyes growing wide. "No way!"

He's looking down at the floor now as if he's interested in the pair of dirty socks partially hidden beneath a magazine, but he nods. "Yep, she did. By the time I heard the accusation, I was pretty much history."

"Didn't you deny it?"

"Of course. But it was her word against mine."

"But I saw her here, Dad. She was obviously here by her own free will. She didn't look harassed to me."

"Well, I couldn't exactly call you in as a witness, especially since you weren't speaking to me at the time."

"So what happened?"

"I agreed to leave my job quietly with a very small severance package, but I can never get a job recommendation from there. Do you know how hard it is to find work without that?"

"So you haven't been working at all?"

"Nope. I have been officially unemployed since shortly before Christmas. I've applied to every place I can think of, but it looks like I'm washed-up around here. I don't think I could even get arrested in this town." Then he leans forward, puts his head in his hands, and actually begins to cry—just quietly, but it cuts right through me just the same.

"I'm sorry, Dad," I tell him. I wish I could go over there and hug him or something, but for the moment, this is the best I can do. "I had no idea. And Mom doesn't know either?"

He looks up and shakes his head. "I know I should've told her, but I figured she'd just laugh in my face. I guess I couldn't take it. I thought I could get hired someplace else and just pretend this never happened."

"So that's why our finances are such a wreck?"

"I traded my Explorer for an old Honda that barely runs. I'll be out of this place by the end of the month."

"What are you going to do?"

"I don't know." Then he sits up straighter. "So tell me, how's your mom doing? Did she take Louisa's death pretty hard?"

"Yeah, you can say that."

"Too bad. How about Elisa and Marc—are they okay?"

"Yeah, I guess."

"But everybody still hates me?"

I shrug.

"I hear your mom has a boyfriend."

I consider that statement—how odd it sounds to have my father saying that about my mother. How did we ever get to this place? "Actually, he hasn't been around too much since Louisa died. I'm hoping Mom is going to lose him."

Dad looks hopeful. "You don't like him?"

"Not at all."

"How about your mom—does she like him?"

"I don't know. I think she likes that he likes her. He's always telling her how pretty she is and stuff like that. She kind of eats that up."

Dad sighs. "Yeah, I can imagine."

Now I look at him for several seconds, this shadow of the dad I once respected and loved. That one seems like a distant memory now. "Why did this happen, Dad? Tia Louisa once told me to get your side of the story, but I figured the only reason you left Mom was because of your affair. Was I right?"

He picks up the dirty socks now, wads them up, and throws them toward the bathroom in the hallway. "You really want the honest answer to that question, Maggie?"

"Yeah, I do."

"You think you're old enough to handle it?"

I consider this. "I'm eighteen, Dad—an adult by some standards."

He nods and then slowly exhales. "Well, during the past few years, your mom and I started to grow apart, you know what I mean? She was getting more and more caught up in her job, and I felt like she was pushing me away all the time—especially when it came to the bedroom."

I feel my cheeks growing warm now and wonder if I really am old enough to hear this. I mean, who wants to listen to the gory details of her parents' sex life? But I remind myself that I asked for this, and I attempt to keep a straight face and just listen.

"I asked her about going to get some help—for our problems, you know—but she didn't see it as a problem. She said it was just how couples our age were supposed to act." He picks up a pillow that's on the floor and gives it a punch. "Well, I just didn't see it that way. I'm sorry, but I wasn't ready to hang it up. I'm only forty-eight, Maggie. That might seem old to you, but there's a lot of life left in this old guy. Anyway, there used to be. I'm not so sure anymore. I'm not sure of much of anything anymore."

I try to process his words, try to understand how this must've made him feel. I remember how I felt when Ned rejected me, how badly it hurt for a while. "So you got involved with Stephanie then?"

"Not right away, Maggie. And like I told you back at the beginning, I never really meant for that to happen."

"Yeah, I'm sure no one ever does, Dad—I mean, not at first anyway. But then you cross this line, don't you? You know it's wrong, but you still step right across it." Even as I say this, I'm remembering that night when I was going to invite Ned to go to a hotel with me, knowing full well that it would be wrong. It was a line I was willing to cross anyway. I'm so thankful I never got the chance.

"I guess you're right, Maggie. You do reach that place where you have to choose, and I chose wrong. And in the process I lost everything." He tightens his hands into fists. "Even God."

"No," I say quickly, "you didn't lose God. You just turned your back on him, Dad. I know because I did the same thing. But when I figured it out, and turned back around, well, he was still there."

"Maybe for you."

"For everyone, Dad. You know that as well as I do."

He looks down at the floor again. "Maybe in my head, but that's where it stops."

"Well, you're the only one who's stopping it, Dad, because God is still there, just waiting for you to figure things out."

He seems to consider this but still appears unconvinced.

"The reason I came over here . . ." I take in a deep breath, telling myself I can do this. I mean, how hard can it be to forgive a guy who's so down on his luck? Even so, I have to pray for help. "The reason I came was to tell you that I forgive you, Dad."

He looks truly surprised now. "Really?"

I nod. "Yes. I know that God wants me to forgive you. And even though I can kind of understand how it might've happened now, I still think you were wrong to cheat on Mom, but I forgive you anyway. And I'm sorry I was so mean to you—that time when I told you that you were dead."

"I think maybe it was prophetic, Maggie, because I do feel dead now." He runs his hands through his hair in an act of pure frustration. "And today, at Louisa's funeral, I was wishing it were me instead. I was wishing I had died back before this stupid thing with Stephanie ever happened. I would rather be dead and buried and remembered with dignity than to be stuck with the mess I've created and have to live with now."

"Maybe that's what you're doing," I say, not even sure why or exactly what I mean. "Maybe you are sort of dying now—not physically, but maybe you're dying to all the crud that you created so that God can give you a new life if you let him."

"I wish that were true."

"You can make it true, Dad, if you take the whole thing to God. You know you can. You know that God is all about forgiveness. Father Thomas said today that forgiveness is the cornerstone of our faith. Without it, the whole foundation crumbles." I can't believe I actually remembered that verbatim.

We talk a while longer, and then I notice it's getting dark and remember I never told Mom where I was going.

"I better get back," I tell him as I stand.

"Thanks for coming, Maggie." He gives me a sad smile. "It means a lot to see you. I hope I can see you again."

"Will you think about what I said?"

"If you promise to keep talking to me."

"It's a deal." And we shake on it.

"Are you going to tell your mom about all this?" He waves his hands. "Losing my job and being broke and useless."

"Do you want me to?"

"I'd rather do it myself."

"Then why don't you?"

He nods. "Maybe I will."

"I'm sure she'll enjoy it."

He kind of laughs. "Yeah, you're probably right about that. She might even throw a party and invite all her friends."

I consider the recent loss of Louisa. "Probably not."

Then we say good-bye, and I drive home thinking that forgiving my dad wasn't nearly as tough as I thought it would be. And it felt good—surprisingly good.

But when I get home, I see Rich's El Camino parked in front of the house and realize that just because I've forgiven Dad doesn't mean life is suddenly going to be all perfect and wonderful again. I'll admit it: Just seeing Dad suffering like that, knowing that he and Stephanie are history, well, I suppose I imagined that this could be a new beginning for my parents—like maybe he'd show up with a dozen roses, get down on his knees, and beg my mom to forgive him. And maybe he will do that sometime, but not tonight.

twenty

"WHAT EXACTLY IS GOING ON WITH YOU AND RICH ANYWAY?" I ASK MY mom about a week after Tia Louisa's funeral. It's Valentine's Day, and she came home from work early and immediately started fixing herself up like she's got some big date tonight. She's wearing a new hot-pink dress and a lethal pair of spike heels, and I can tell she's just had her roots touched up. Meanwhile, Rich is sitting downstairs watching TV.

"What do you mean?" she asks as she applies a shade of lipstick that I'm sure was chosen specially for the dress.

"I'm just curious about you and Rich. I mean, he's becoming a permanent fixture in our house. Like, doesn't he have a home of his own?"

"Maggie!"

"Okay, sorry. But I want to know what's going on with you guys."

"What do you mean?" she asks again, which irritates me because I'm sure I'm being pretty clear, and it reveals just how muddled my mom's thinking is getting.

"I *mean* are you guys getting serious?"

She laughs as she squirts some mousse into her hands and rubs it into her hair. "Serious?"

"Yeah, serious. I mean, do you really like him? As in are you considering marrying him? Because you might as well know right up front that none of us kids, including Marc and Elisa, likes him. So if you're thinking Rich is going to be our new daddy, well, you might want to think again."

"So you kids sit around discussing my love life, do you?" Her eyes are starting to spark now, like I might've gone a bit too far.

"We talked about it a little, Mom—last weekend, you know. They were curious as to what you saw in him. I am too."

"He's nice to me, Maggie. Is it so wrong for me to enjoy being in the company of a man who's nice to me?"

"But you know why he's nice to you, Mom? I mean, you're not dumb."

She gives me a sharp sideways glance as she applies some jet-black mascara. "What are you saying?"

"You know what I'm saying, Mom. What do you think he's interested in? In other words, are his intentions honorable?"

This makes her laugh.

"I'm serious, Mom. I can tell by the way he looks at you that he wants to sleep with you. Don't tell me you don't know that."

She shrugs. "That's the way men are, little girl. The sooner you figure that one out, the smarter you'll be."

"I've already figured *that* one out," I tell her in exasperation. "I'm just relieved that you have too."

"I'm a grown woman, Maggie. You don't need to worry about me."

"Fine," I say. "Don't say I didn't warn you."

Then my mom informs me that she and Rich are driving over to Lamberg. "To that lovely restaurant," she says as she liberally sprays herself with perfume that smells like rotten flowers. Ea de Pew Pew.

"You mean the one at that lovely *inn*?" I add. "So do you plan to spend the night, then?"

"Oh, Maggie." She frowns at me with the same expression she might've used when I was five years old and had just spilled red punch all over my new Easter dress.

And so I give up. "Have a lovely evening." I let my voice drip sarcasm.

I drive to work later figuring she's utterly hopeless. It's Mom's life, not mine, and if she wants to make a total mess of it, there's not much I can do. Fortunately, I have only a few more months until graduation, and if she does something really stupid, like marry Rich, I can always move out.

It's the first night the restaurant's been open since Tia Louisa died. As a result, everyone is pretty quiet and somber to start with, and I notice that a few more tears are shed, including my own when I walk past her office and see the door closed with a black wreath hanging on it. I still can't believe she's gone or how much I miss her. I feel sad to think of all those years when I never really knew her that well or that I actually used to be afraid of her. How I wish she were still here, still giving me wise words of advice.

Fortunately, it's Valentine's Day and the place gets so busy that we don't have much time to dwell in the sadness, and by the end of the night it feels as if we've managed a successful comeback. I imagine Tia Louisa up there in heaven smiling down on us or maybe even applauding. Casa del Sol lives on.

I'm not too surprised that Mom isn't home when I get back. After all, it's not even eleven. But I am a little surprised when she's not here the next morning. I'm also a little worried. The first thing I imagine is that Rich's stupid El Camino hit ice on one of those hairpin curves and that he and Mom have both been killed, or maybe he's dead and she's pinned in his car. But I realize that I'm just being melodramatic and that they're probably perfectly fine. Just the same, I listen to the local morning news on the radio to make sure there haven't been any bad wrecks.

I'm tempted to call Mom's cell phone when it's nearly noon and I still haven't heard anything, but at the same time I am feeling seriously angry. Like, why should the kid be checking up on the mom? Besides, if they actually did spend the night together, like it appears they did, I'd rather not speak to her right now. I might say something really nasty and horrible.

Suddenly I remember that I promised to meet Dad for coffee today at one. I'm not really looking forward to this, especially when I remember how down-and-out he seemed last week. Talk about depressing. But, I tell myself, he probably needs me now. And I know he hasn't talked to Mom yet—hasn't informed her of his unfortunate state of affairs, or nonaffairs—because I'm sure Mom would've been beside herself with joy to hear what a miserable wretch he has become. I was tempted to spill the beans myself, but now that she's gone and done what I'm fairly sure that she went and did, well, I'm not so sure.

Dad and I meet at Starbucks. I think Dad's too embarrassed to go to Java Hut after the scene I made last time. I'm relieved to see that Dad looks more like himself today. He has on clean clothes, is shaved, and even looks slightly happy to see me.

We order our coffee and sit down, and straightaway he tells me that he got a job. "It's not much," he says. "Just sales at JD Mischlers, but I think it could turn into something. I was completely honest with the personnel director, and when I interviewed with the VP, he said that something like that had happened to him once. He was willing to give me a chance."

I smile. "That's great, Dad. Congratulations."

"I'll be making only about half of what I used to make, but it's better than nothing, right?"

"Definitely. So are you going to stay in your town house, then?"

"I don't know." He frowns. "I already gave notice, and I think I should look for something cheaper." Now he brightens. "How's your mom doing? Is she getting over the loss of her sister?"

I'm sure my expression is a dead giveaway. It's a well-known fact that I should never play poker.

"What's wrong?" he asks.

"Oh, nothing."

"Come on, Maggie. You can tell me. I've already told you all my secrets."

So I tell him about Rich and Mom and where they went last night and how she didn't come home.

He sighs and looks down at his coffee. "I guess I shouldn't be surprised."

"Are you disappointed?" I ask. "Hurt?"

He nods. "Yeah. But I had this coming. She never would've done this if I hadn't messed up, Maggie. You really can't blame her."

I'm not so sure that I agree with him on this, at least not completely. I mean, Mom made her own choice. No one forced her to go out with Rich—or to spend the night with him.

"I just wish you had talked to her last week," I tell him, my frustration showing. "I mean, maybe it would've made a difference."

"I tried to," he says sadly. "I left her a couple of messages, but she never called back. She probably assumed it had to do with the divorce and the lawyers since that's about all we talk about, and that usually just amounts to yelling and accusing." He shakes his head. "Not very pretty."

"I know."

"So she's serious about this Rich guy?"

I roll my eyes. "Seems that way."

"Well, maybe that's for the best, Maggie. Your mom deserves a good guy."

"A good guy?" I kind of laugh. "Elisa and Marc and I all think he's a sleazebucket."

"A sleazebucket?"

"Yeah. We can't stand him." Then I give him the full description. "He's so lame, Dad, with all his gold jewelry and that ridiculous El Camino. It's totally humiliating. And if they decide to get married, I am like so out of there."

Dad actually laughs now.

"I'm serious. This dude is bad news. And he practically lives at our house. I can't wait to graduate so I can move out."

Dad gets thoughtful. "You know that if it gets really bad, Maggie, you can always come live with me. I might keep the town house if I thought you needed a place to stay."

"Seriously?"

"Yeah. Not that I want to come between you and your mom, but if it would help you finish out your senior year, you know you'd be more than welcome."

"I'll keep that in mind. And if Rich starts spending the night or anything like that, well, I might take you up on that offer."

"So it sounds like your mom has completely fallen away from her faith too." Dad looks as though he's on the verge of tears now. "And that would also be my fault. I can't believe how bad I've messed up this family."

I consider this. "There are a lot of things you can blame your-self for, Dad, like as far as messing up your marriage and stuff, but I think when it comes to any of us and our faith, well, that's the result of our own personal choices, and you can't take the blame for that. If Mom walked away from God, it was her decision, not yours. I know it was my choice when I walked away, and it was my choice to turn around and walk back. I might've tried to blame that on you, but that was just an excuse."

"That may be true, but still, I've been a pretty lousy spiritual leader."

Okay, I guess I can't argue with that, I silently agree.

"And I really doubt that your mom would've gotten involved with this Rich character if I had stuck around."

"Yeah," I say, "that's probably true."

"So what can I do about it?" He looks at me as if I should have the answer.

"I don't know. All I can tell you is that you better take care of your own life, Dad. I mean, when it comes to getting your heart right with God, that's about all you can do right now. Get right with God and see what he wants you to do. That's what I'm trying to do."

"I've been thinking about that sermon you gave me last week."

"Sermon?"

"About forgiveness."

"You mean Father Thomas's sermon."

"Right. Anyway, I know what you said is true. And I'm trying to get back to that place, Maggie. It's just not easy. I have a boat-load of guilt to deal with."

"Why don't you come to church with me tomorrow?"

He looks surprised. "To our old church?"

"Yeah, why not?"

He frowns. "Isn't it your mother's church? I hate to infringe."

"It's not like she's been going, Dad. Seriously, she hasn't been there since Christmas, and that was only because Elisa insisted we go."

"I guess I could go."

"We could go together, Dad. I'll even pick you up if you want."

He smiles. "Okay, then, let's do it. It's a date."

With that settled, I tell Dad I need to go home to get ready for work. I don't mention that I also feel the need to check on Mom and make sure she's okay. I mean, how pathetic is that?

"See you tomorrow," he calls as we head for our cars.

And as I drive home, I'm thinking maybe there is hope after all. Maybe my parents aren't totally a lost cause. But then I see Rich's El Camino in the driveway—without a scratch or dent on it—and I want to scream.

I walk past the kitchen, where Mom and Rich are getting something to eat, and head straight upstairs. I ignore my mom's greeting and Rich's "hey" as I go into my room and slam my door. Okay, maybe I am acting juvenile, but then I am the kid here, right?

The next thing I know, Mom is knocking on my door.

"What?" I demand when I open it.

"While you are living in my house, under my roof, you will show a little respect, young lady. Rich and I both said hello to you, and you were extremely rude."

"Respect?" I practically spit the word out at her. "Why should I respect you, Mom? Where were you last night? Why didn't you call? Do you consider yourself respectable?"

Her loss of words convinces me that my assumption is correct and, at the same time, it makes me feel sick.

She narrows her eyes now. "Don't judge me, Magdela."

"I wonder what Tia Louisa would think of her baby sister now," I say, instantly wishing I hadn't.

Mom looks like I cut her to the heart. I see tears in her eyes, but she just turns away and stomps off. I know I should say that I'm sorry, but the words get stuck in my throat.

I quickly dress for work and leave without speaking to either of them. I wouldn't be surprised if Mom changes the locks again while I'm gone. I have a feeling I may have to take Dad up on his offer to live with him sooner than I'd planned.

I feel miserable as I work, and I know that I have blown it big-time. Yet at the same time, I feel this deep sense of indignation, like it's Mom's fault for sleeping with Rich. How can she expect me to respect her after that?

Realizing I can't go home under these circumstances and not really wanting to explain the situation to Dad, I call Claire during my break and ask if I can crash at her house tonight.

"Sure," she tells me. "It seems like we haven't really talked in ages."

So after work I go to Claire's, and trying to be somewhat responsible, I actually call home and leave a message. Then I dump all my latest crud onto Claire, and she listens patiently.

"Wow," she says when I finish. "I can't believe your mom really did that. It is so unlike her."

I shrug. "I don't know. It's like my parents weren't really who I thought they were in the first place anyway. It's like everything in my life is upside down, and I'm not sure what to expect." Then I tell her about Dad and how he agreed to go to church with me.

"That's great, Maggie. So your dad is really coming back around, then?"

"I guess."

"Then maybe they'll get back together."

"I don't really think so—I mean, not with the way Mom is acting. It's like they're just totally out of sync. Maybe God never meant them to be together in the first place, Claire. Maybe it was just a big mistake right from the start." But even as I say this, I don't think it's really true.

"Well, really all you can do is take care of yourself, you know."

I nod. "Yeah, I think you're right about that."

twenty-one

I FEEL AS THOUGH I DON'T EVEN KNOW MY MOM ANYMORE. IT'S AS IF she's turned into someone else, someone I don't like and cannot respect.

Dad, on the other hand, seems to be turning back into his old self, only better. He seems more humble and human and understanding now. And he keeps telling me I need to forgive Mom.

"I know you're right," I tell him at lunch after church. It's the second time he's been back to church, and he says he plans to keep going. "I've been asking God to help me forgive her, and sometimes I think I almost have, but then I see her with Rich and . . ." I make a groaning sound. "It's like I'm stuck."

"Well, it might take time."

"Dad," I begin, "remember your offer? For me to move in?"

"Sure. You need to take me up on it?"

"Maybe so."

"Because of Rich?"

I nod, trying to hold back the tears burning in the back of my eyes. "I know they think I don't know, and they're being really sneaky and quiet, but I know he's spent the night, and it just makes me feel so uncomfortable, like it's not even my home anymore. I get up in the morning and there he is, reading the paper as if he belongs there more than I do." Now the tears come. "And I just can't take it, Dad."

"I understand. Move in anytime you like." Then he gets a thoughtful expression. "Just try to do it right, Maggie—for your sake and for your mom's."

Do it right? How do I do it right? Is there a right way to tell your mother that you don't know her anymore, that you can't stand how she's living, that you no longer feel at home in your own house? I don't think so. Even so, I tell Dad that I'll do my best.

So I go home after lunch and begin to pack my things. I find some boxes in the garage, along with some big trash bags, and before long, my car is stuffed with most of my belongings. I'm not sure where Mom is, but since her car is still here, I'm assuming she's with Rich. To be honest, I'm not even sure they came home last night, since I went to bed before I ever heard them and when I got up the house was quiet, which was actually preferable to having Rich in the kitchen drinking coffee like he owns the place.

I wait around for a while and even think about leaving a note, but then that seems pretty impersonal and cold. I decide I'll just call her later, after I get settled in at Dad's place.

I'm just getting into my car when she and Rich pull up, and she immediately sees my loaded-down car and hops out of the El Camino and comes marching toward me.

"What are you doing?" she demands.

"I'm moving in with Dad," I say in a calm voice.

"Just like that?" She glares at me. "Sneaking away while I'm gone? Not even planning to tell me?"

"I planned to tell you, Mom, but you weren't here. I was going to—"

"It figures!" she snaps. "You're just like your father. Well, fine, go then. See if I care." And then she walks away.

I am trying not to cry as I drive across town, trying not to replay the hatred that I'm sure I saw in her eyes. But I remember something Ned told me once—about how he feels torn between his parents, how it's hard to choose which ones to spend holidays with. And while I know that Dad's not pulling at me right now, I realize what a minefield this might turn into some day, and it's disheartening.

Two weeks pass rather uneventfully, and I don't see or talk to my mom once. But here's what's weird: As much as I feel that I don't like her or know her, I find that I do miss her. But it's the *old* her I miss, not this new person, Rich's girlfriend. I think as much as I've been grieving the loss of Tia Louisa, I am also grieving the loss of my mother. Will this ever end?

"We met with the divorce attorneys today," Dad announces as I make a salad. We're both helping to make dinners these days. Dad thought it wasn't fair to put the full burden on me, and I really do appreciate that.

"How did it go?" I ask as I slice a tomato.

He moans. "Not so great."

Then he tells me about how Mom is going for everything. "She wants the house, wants me to pay off her car, wants alimony, the works."

"So hearing about your circumstances didn't really soften her up?" I ask as I start to peel a cucumber. I know that last week Dad finally told her about losing his job, breaking up with Stephanie, and all the other crud. He thought it might help her to be more understanding when it came time to negotiate some kind of out-of-court settlement.

"Apparently not."

"So will the divorce have to go to court?" I ask.

"Unless she backs down on some things." He dumps the pasta into the boiling water. "She's asking for more than I can possibly give, and it might take a judge to explain it to her. Unfortunately, that will end up costing us both a lot of money, without much to be gained."

"That's too bad." I don't remind him that it's costing us all a lot, and more than just money too. He knows that already.

"Yeah. I wish she could see that she's creating a lose-lose situation."

"Do you think it would help if I talked to her?"

Dad frowns. "I don't want you caught in the middle of this, Maggie."

I have to laugh. "It's a little late for that."

"Well, do what you think is right." He pauses. "And be sure to pray about it first."

"Yeah." I toss the salad ingredients together. "I have been. And I think the time has come for me to tell Mom that I'm sorry and that I forgive her."

He smiles now. "That's good to hear, Maggie. I know you're going to feel a lot better when you take care of that. I sure did."

"You told Mom you were sorry?"

"Lots of times."

"But she hasn't forgiven you?"

"Not yet."

"Not yet?"

"She'll come around, Maggie—eventually. She's a good woman—a good woman who's been deeply hurt. That's my fault."

So I stop by Mom's office after school the next day. I realize I probably should've called first since she could be in a meeting or out showing a house, but I find her sitting in her office thumbing through a big stack of papers.

"Maggie!" she looks up in surprise.

"Hi, Mom."

"What's wrong?"

"Nothing." I sit down. "I just want to talk. Do you have a few minutes?"

"Sure." She gets up and closes the door, sitting down in the chair beside me. "Are you okay?"

The sincerity in her voice gets to me. It reminds me of who she used to be, the mom I've been missing.

"I just want to tell you"—my voice breaks now—"that I'm sorry, Mom. I said some mean things to you, and I know that I hurt you, and I'm sorry."

"Oh, *mi hija!*" she exclaims, hugging me. "I'm sorry too."

"And I've missed you," I tell her.

"I've missed you too."

Tears are coming now. "And I want you to know that I forgive you too. I mean, you probably don't even know why, but the truth is, I've been really mad at you about Rich, and I realize that I can't hold it against you anymore and I need to forgive you."

And then we just hug and cry for a little while. Finally, we let go, and Mom digs a box of tissues out of her desk so we can wipe our eyes.

"Are you moving back home now?" she asks hopefully.

I don't know what to say. I hadn't even considered this possibility. Finally, I ask about Rich. "Are you guys still together?"

She nods, tossing her used tissue into the wastebasket and sitting a little straighter. "Is that a problem?"

"It just makes me uncomfortable," I admit.

She frowns. "I don't know why you're so hard on him, Maggie. You should get to know him. You might even like him."

While I seriously doubt this, I just nod, acting like she might be right. I still have serious misgivings about El Camino Man. "Yeah, I suppose I've been judging him," I say, "and I'm sure you wouldn't like him if he were a jerk."

She laughs now. "Don't be so sure. I liked your father, and he was a jerk."

I feel like I need to bite my tongue now.

"So how's it going with him?" she asks. "Did he come home all angry about the meeting yesterday?"

"No, not angry—just sad mostly."

She rolls her eyes. "I can just imagine."

"Really, Mom. He totally regrets this whole mess."

"It's his mess, Maggie."

"I know. He knows. But how is he supposed to clean it up? I mean, you're not exactly being reasonable. Aren't you ever going to forgive him, Mom?"

She crosses her arms across her front, leaning against her desk with a hard-to-read expression. "I don't know, Maggie. I don't know if I ever can."

I nod. "Right. I understand that. Sometimes it's a matter of timing. But then eventually you have to choose, Mom. Eventually you have to decide to forgive."

"Maybe so, but I'm not ready to do it yet."

So then I try to calmly discuss the divorce settlement, trying to make her see that taking their problems to court will only waste money, and suddenly her eyes are flashing at me again, and I can see she is getting angry.

"Your father sent you here, didn't he?"

"No, Mom, I came because—"

"No, he sent you. He thought you would soften me up—that I'd agree to his stupid settlement. Well, tell him he can just forget it, Maggie! And tell him that he should act like a grown man and fight his own battles. And tell him that I will see him in court!" And then she resorted to swearing in Spanish, and I told her I had to go.

Her words still stung as I drove home, they stung as I got ready for work, and they stung as I drove to Casa del Sol. But then I remembered my choice to forgive her, and I realized I would have to forgive her all over again. So I asked God to help me, and I asked him to take the sting of her words away. And by the time I parked my car and walked into the restaurant, I felt a little bit better.

Later as I drove home from work, I realized that without forgiveness we would all live very unhappy lives. Without forgiveness we would all become bitter and jaded and mean. And without forgiveness my mother would never be happy again.

"God help her," I prayed as I parked my car in front of the town house. "Help her to forgive and move on."

twenty-two

GRADUATION IS JUST TWO WEEKS AWAY NOW. THE DIVORCE IS FINAL. MY mom finally agreed to a settlement, so my parents didn't have to go to court. It wasn't the settlement that Dad's lawyer wanted, but it also wasn't the settlement that took everything. Mom sold the house and moved into a condo with Rich. My grandmother isn't speaking to her, and the rest of the family doesn't know what to think. I wonder what Tia Louisa would say. I'm guessing she would calmly tell Mom to get her act together, and then if my mom refused, my aunt would probably still love her anyway.

That's what I'm trying to do, although it's not easy.

Elisa and Marc are still in shock. They both figured that Rich was just a bad phase, Mom's knee-jerk reaction to Dad's unfaithfulness. Turns out they were wrong.

"I don't care what Mom says," Elisa tells me, "that man is not coming to my wedding." Elisa got engaged in April, totally out of the blue, to a guy she's known only since Christmas. The wedding is set for September, but due to our family's problems, Elisa might just elope. "It'll save money," she assures me.

"But what about the rest of the family?" I ask. "Don't you think we'd enjoy a wedding? And it doesn't have to be really expensive.

You know how our relatives love to cook. Hey, maybe you could have the reception at the restaurant."

"I'll think about it," she says, "but I'm still not talking to Mom."

Marc still blames Dad for the divorce. If one has to cast blame, I suppose Dad's the most obvious target, and he certainly doesn't deny his responsibility. In fact, he feels the pain of his mistake almost daily. And he's apologized to everyone more than once. I think, in time, Marc will forgive him. Probably a lot sooner than Mom ever will, although Dad seems certain that she will forgive him eventually.

I still get mad sometimes. I get angry that my parents' choices and mistakes have altered our family forever. And it bugs me that I don't have a "real home" to go back to. I mean, it's nice living here with Dad, and now that it's warm out, I've been enjoying the pool. But I think about going away to college, and I wonder what I'll do for holidays, vacations, and, like Elisa, what I will do if I ever decide to get married. Who will I invite? Who will be blacklisted? Or is God's grace big enough to cover everyone? That's what I'm hoping.

I've been trying to get to know Rich, and I've learned that he actually has some good traits—like he's very loyal to his mother, who still lives in Mexico. He sends her money every month. He's pretty much what you'd call a self-made man, since he came to this country with nothing more than the clothes on his back about thirty years ago. He taught himself English, put himself through school, and then got his Realtor's license. So really, who am I to judge him? Even if I don't like his choice of automobiles or bling bling.

I've also learned that relationships are really important—and fragile—and if I ever get married (I'm still not too sure I will), I want to be certain that I'm marrying a godly man, the man God wants me to marry. And then I want to do everything possible to respect my marriage and make sure that my marriage succeeds because I never, never want to go through what my parents have been through.

Mostly, though, what I've learned through this whole divorce thing is that I have to take responsibility for myself. I have to look over my own spiritual health, my own emotional well-being. And I can't blame my bad choices on other people's mistakes. I have to stand on my own two feet because when I stand before God, he won't be asking me whether my parents had a good marriage; he'll be asking me about myself and whether I really believed in him, trusted in him, and lived my life for him. And that's what I'm trying to do.

reader's guide

1. Why do you think Maggie was so devastated by the news that her parents' marriage was in trouble? How would you feel in similar circumstances?

2. If you were Maggie's friend, what would you have said to her in the early stages of her parents' breakup to encourage her?

3. In the beginning, Maggie's concerns about her parents' problems seemed self-centered (for example, feeling as though her parents were ruining her life). Why do you think she felt that way?

4. Were you surprised to discover that Maggie's dad was having an affair? Why or why not?

5. When Maggie went to work for Tia Louisa, she became part of the restaurant family. Do you think this was good or bad? Why?

6. Maggie often seemed caught in the middle of her parents' battles. How would you handle something like that?

7. Why do you think Maggie's mother was so bitter over the breakup of her marriage? Do you think Rosa will ever forgive Roberto? Why or why not?

8. What did you think of Tia Louisa's influence on Maggie's life? How did you feel when she died?

9. What were some things that Maggie learned about life and relationships as she worked her way through her parents' divorce?

10. Where did Maggie find strength to get through the trying times of her family's breakup? Where do you find your own strength for your own tough times?

TrueColors Book 9:

Faded Denim

Coming in July 2006

*God, why am I so ugly? Why am I so boring and blah
and mousy-looking? Why? Why? Why?*

One

MY BEST FRIEND IS SO SKINNY. *I HATE HER*. NO, NOT REALLY. I LOVE HER.
No, I hate her. The truth is, I think I hate myself. And I hate feel-
ing like this, like I am fat and ugly and a total loser with a capital
L. It makes me sick.

But here's what really makes me just scratch my head and
go *huh?* When did all this happen? When did I fall asleep and
get abducted by the body switchers who did some mean sci-fi
number on me, transforming me into this . . . this *repulsive blob
girl*? I mean, I didn't used to be like this. Back in middle school, I
was super thin. Okay, maybe I was just average thin, but my best
friend, Leah, was, hmmm, shall we say, somewhat pudgy, slightly
overweight, a bit obese, downright chubby?

This is the deal: When I was about thirteen, I reached my present height, which is about five foot seven (that is, if I stand extremely straight and stretch my neck until I hear my spinal column popping). Meanwhile, my friend Leah was about four inches shorter than me, and she weighed about twenty pounds more than me. She was a regular little roly-poly back then, but in the past couple of years she got really tall, and now she's like five foot ten or maybe more and skinny as a stick—so sickeningly skinny that clothes look absolutely fantastic on her. And it just makes me wanna pull my hair out and scream! Or just hide.

Okay, to be fair (to me), I wouldn't feel so miserable about all this if Leah weren't so obsessed with weight and diet and exercise and health that it's begun to feel like she's constantly throwing the whole thing in my face. She says stuff like, "Emily, are you sure you want to eat that Snickers bar, since it has like five hundred calories that will probably end up right on your thighs?" And when she says things like that, it not only makes me want to pig out on the Snickers bar but go grab a giant bag of Cheetos as well. Like supersize me, please!

But that's not the only problem. I mean, since she got all tall and thin (and did I mention gorgeous?), she's also gotten into fashion and beauty tricks and the latest, according to her, styles. She studies all the fashion rags, which, of course, feature these tall, bony, weird-looking models who really do look a bit like aliens, if you ask me—probably a product of the body switchers. Leah has recently decided she actually wants to become one of them. At first I thought she was kidding.

"You seriously would want to put yourself in that position?" I asked her, incredulous. "I mean, you want perfect strangers gaping at your body while you strut around in some weird outfit, possibly with no underwear on?"

"I think it'd be cool." And the mind-boggling part is that she really believes she could make it as a fashion runway model. They, according to her, are the ones who make megabucks, although I've also heard that lots of them wind up strung out on drugs and are generally messed up by the time they're twenty.

"That doesn't happen to everyone," she told me after I mentioned my concerns. "Those are just the girls who make the news and the tabloids and then everyone assumes it's the whole fashion industry that's at fault. And that's not fair."

Of course, it doesn't help matters that her aunt is a well-established fashion photographer in New York City or that she actually thinks Leah may "have what it takes." I'm sure that aunts are a lot like moms and most likely are easily duped into thinking their kids "have what it takes" to do just about anything. Yeah, right.

"Okay, what *does* it take?" I asked Leah several weeks ago. (This was shortly after she convinced me to go on this stupid cabbage-soup diet that was guaranteed to take off a few pounds but in reality nearly killed me. I ended up in the john for like an entire afternoon. What a fun diet!)

"What does it take to be a runway model?" She pressed her full lips together as she considered my question. "Well, it obviously takes some height, and you have to be pretty thin . . . and you need good bone structure, even features . . . and then, of course, you have to have that special something."

"Special something," I said hopefully. Now, I may not look like a runway model, but I am good at making friends and making them laugh. Some people think that's pretty special. Naturally, I don't say this.

"Yeah, kind of like personality, only more than that—it has to be something that cameras can catch, especially if you're going the print route. Otherwise you need that something extra that shows from the runway—an attitude, you know. You gotta be able to strut your stuff and make people want what you have."

"Right." I nodded as if I understood, but more and more it feels like Leah is speaking a foreign language and I am struggling just to keep up.

"I get to see my portfolio shots on Friday afternoon," she told me a few days ago. "Want to go with me to pick out the ones I'll use?"

"Sure," I offered, having absolutely no idea what I was getting myself into.

So here we are at this fancy-schmancy modeling agency, where all the girls are tall, thin, and fabulous, and I feel like a creature from another planet—the planet where the body switchers dwell. Uranus, perhaps.

"Ooh," gushes Becca (a Scandinavian-looking blonde). She seems to know Leah and has just joined us to look at the photos. "That's totally scrumptious, Leah." Becca is pointing a perfectly sculpted nail to a shot of Leah, which in my opinion is exposing way too much cleavage, but naturally I don't mention this. I just stand there where these glossy photos are spread all over the counter and try to keep up.

Mostly I wish I could blend in with the aluminum-looking wallpapered walls, which in reality must make me stand out even more in my "fat" jeans (okay, I was bloated today), and I also have on this old hoodie sweatshirt that is baggy enough to cover a multitude of sins, although I'm sure it simply makes me look like a cow. I try to shrink away from these two girls, seriously wishing I could just vanish.

"Is there, uh, a restroom around?" I ask meekly.

"Yeah," Leah jerks her thumb to the left. "Down that hallway, on the right."

And then I slink away, feeling dumpy and dowdy and just plain pathetic. I consider leaving this plastic place and going home, except that Leah is the one who drove us here, and I can't exactly steal her car, although I do know where her spare key is hidden in its little magnetic box under the right fender. But instead of committing grand larceny, I just go into the bathroom and spend enough time in the john to make someone think I have a serious bowel disorder. In reality, I sit and read a fashion magazine that someone left on the counter. Okay, call me a glutton for punishment.

When I finally glance at my watch, I see it's nearly five o'clock, and I'm hopeful that this place will be closing soon. Then I can walk out of the bathroom, we can go home, and I can forget all about this. I emerge from the john and take an inordinate amount of time washing my hands, the whole while staring at my pitifully disappointing reflection.

This is what I would call very unforgiving light—a garishly bright strip right above the enormous mirror. I'm sure it's there so that models can come in here and carefully examine themselves to detect if there are any possible flaws (like they have any), and then I'm sure they do their best to address these minor blips before their next big photo shoot. But as I stand here gaping at my lackluster reflection, my dull brown hair (which needs washing), and my boring brown eyes, I suddenly notice that a new zit is about to erupt on my chin. I want to cry.

"God, why am I so ugly?" I actually mutter out loud, quickly glancing over my shoulder toward the three stalls to see if any feet (which would be adorned in the coolest footwear, I'm certain) are present. Thank goodness there are not.

Even so, I continue my line of questioning silently. (I really was addressing God, not just taking his name in vain.) I ask my Maker what he could've been thinking when he made a loser like me.

Why do I look like this? Why is my nose so long? Why am I short and fat? Why is my hair plain and brown? Maybe I should consider highlighting it, as Leah has suggested. Why am I so boring and blah and mousy-looking? Why? Why? Why?

"Hey, Emily," says Leah as she comes in with a big black folder, which I assume is her portfolio. "I've been looking for you. Are you okay?"

I blink back what threaten to become real tears and force a smile. "Yeah, I'm fine. What's up?"

"Becca helped me to pick out the photos, but you were in here so long I was worried that you might be sick or something—like maybe you've been eating that cabbage soup again." She chuckled. "Really, are you okay?"

"I'm fine," I say again, knowing it's a big fat lie. Then I point to her portfolio. "So are they really great? Going to launch your big career in New York?"

She laughs. "Not quite, but it's a start. LaMar says that he might have a job for me next weekend." She smirks. "Okay, it's only a Mother's Day fashion show, but hey, it's better than nothing, right?"

I nod. "Right. That's great, Leah. Congratulations!"

And as she drives me home, she gushes about how cool the agency is, and then she changes gears and starts telling me about this new cream that Becca was just telling her about that's supposed to make your thighs thinner.

"Hey, maybe you should try it," she says suddenly, turning and looking at me as if I should become some kind of science experiment for her and her new model pals.

"Try what?" I say, pretending that I wasn't really listening. I had been partially daydreaming anyway, or maybe I just want to appear slightly brain-dead when it comes to all her mind-numbing beauty talk.

"That thigh cream." She goes on to tell me what it's called and how you have to get it online and on and on and on.

I am so thankful when she gets to my house. "Thanks," I tell her, wondering what exactly I'm thanking her for: the ride or the torture?

"Oh, yeah," she says suddenly, "I almost forgot to tell you something." Now she has this mysterious expression on her face, like she's got some big secret. Despite my wanting to escape her, I am pulled in.

"What?"

"In all the excitement of getting my photos, I almost forgot to tell you about Brett McEwen."

"What about Brett McEwen?"

"He asked me to prom!" She shrieks loudly enough that every-one in my neighborhood can probably hear her.

"No way!" The truth is, this really is shocking news. I mean, Brett McEwen is a pretty cool guy. And not only is he cool, he's fairly nice too. But he's never really given Leah (or me) a second look before. I mean, sure, he says hey to us and even chats with us now and then (which I assume he feels compelled to do, since we all go to the same youth group). But asking Leah to prom . . . well, this is mind-blowing.

She nods, grinning and exposing her perfectly straight teeth, which she got whitened right after the braces came off last fall. "Way!"

"Wow." I just shake my head in amazement.

"I am so totally jazzed. I can hardly believe it."

"Yeah, I can imagine." And the sad thing is that I *can* imagine. I mean, I've imagined myself going out—not to prom but just someplace ordinary—with Brett McEwen. He's been my secret (like really, really secret—even Leah doesn't know) crush since freshman year.

"At first I actually thought he was kidding me," she's telling me now. "I was like, 'Okay, Brett, don't be stringing me along here. I know that you can't be serious.'"

"But he was?"

"Yes! He said that he'd been thinking about asking me out for a few months now but that he couldn't get up the nerve." She shrieks again. "*The nerve!* Can you believe that? Like he was intimidated by *me*?"

"Well, you *are* trying to become a supermodel, Leah. Maybe the word's getting around."

She laughs loudly. "Yeah, right. Last year's nerd girl finally thinks she's got it together."

"You weren't exactly last year's nerd girl," I protest.

"No, just brace-faced, kinky-haired, gangly, big-footed Leah Clark. Not exactly Jessica Simpson, if you know what I mean."

"Well, the ugly ducking has turned into a swan," I say, trying to sound more positive than I feel.

Her smile grows even bigger. "Sometimes I can't even believe it myself, Emily. It's like I look in the mirror and have to pinch myself."

"I'll bet."

"Not that I'm perfect," she continues as I lean half-in and half-out of her Honda. My back is starting to ache from this frozen position. "I mean, especially after looking at some of those photos today." She makes a face. "Some of them were really awful, but like Becca said, it's a good way to see the things that need to be addressed."

"Addressed?"

"Yeah." She nods with enthusiasm. "You know, like with the right makeup or airbrushing and maybe even a little surgery. A little nip and tuck."

"Like, I'm sure, Leah. Why on earth would *you* ever consider surgery?"

"Hey, I'm thinking about it. But I have to talk to Aunt Cassie first."

"What could you possibly need surgery for?" I ask.

"A breast reduction. Duh."

I blink and then look at her chest. "But why?"

"Because they're too big, silly."

"They're not *that* big, Leah. What are you? Like a B cup?"

She laughs. "I wish. No, I'm actually a C. Can you believe it? I mean, like just last year I could barely fit into a double A. And it's not like I've put on any weight either. In fact, I weigh less now than I did as a sophomore. Grandma Morris says it's genetics, from her side of the family. I guess my mom had them too—not that I can remember." Leah sighs.

Her mom died when she was six. I can barely remember her myself, but I can't help but wonder what her mother would think of the idea of her daughter wanting to get breast-reduction surgery when she's only seventeen. I know my mom would totally freak, but then, she didn't even want me to get my ears pierced. Fortunately, I talked her into it, but not until I turned sixteen. Talk about old-fashioned!

"Well, tell me what your aunt says," I say, standing up now. "And if you want my opinion, I say don't do it."

She laughs. "Yeah, big surprise there, Em."

"Seriously," I tell her. "I've seen models who've gotten implants just so that they can be as big as you. Why would you want to go the other direction? I mean, you look great, Leah." Then I laugh. "If you don't believe me, maybe you should ask Brett McEwen. I'm sure he'd have an opinion."

Now she gets a serious look. "Do *not* tell anyone about this conversation," she warns me. "Besides, if I do it, it won't be until summer, and I don't want anyone to know, okay?"

I dramatically press a forefinger to my lips. "Mum's the word."

"Thanks."

"But, just for the record, Leah, I think your boobs are perfectly fine!" Then I slam the door and head up to my house. *Breast-reduction surgery!* Get real.

And okay, as I open the front door, I am starting to feel angry—really, really angry. I'm not sure whether I'm angry at Leah for being so skinny and gorgeous and having a prom date with Brett, or just angry at myself for not. Or maybe I'm angry at God for making me like this in the first place. But as I stomp up the stairs to my room, I seriously feel like breaking something!

about the author

MELODY CARLSON has written dozens of books for all age groups, but she particularly enjoys writing for teens. Perhaps this is because her own teen years remain so vivid in her memory. After claiming to be an atheist at the ripe old age of twelve, she later surrendered her heart to Jesus and has been following him ever since. Her hope and prayer for all of her readers is that each one would be touched by God in a special way through her stories. For more information, please visit Melody's website at www.melodycarlson.com.

DISCOVER A UNIQUE NEW KIND OF BIBLE STUDY.

How did Jesus teach many of his most important lessons? He told stories. That's the idea behind the first series of Bible studies from best-selling fiction author Melody Carlson. In each of the four studies, Melody weaves fictional stories with practical discussion questions to get you thinking about some of the most important topics in life: your relationship with God, your relationship with others, identity, and forgiveness.

Knowing God Better Than Ever
1-57683-725-4

Finding Out Who You Really Are
1-57683-726-2

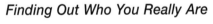

Making the Most of Your Relationships
1-57683-727-0

Discovering a Forgiveness Plan
1-57683-728-9

ALSO FROM MELODY CARLSON

Dark Blue: *Color Me Lonely*

Brutally ditched by her best friend, Kara feels totally abandoned until she discovers that these dark blue days contain a life-changing secret.

1-57683-529-4

Deep Green: *Color Me Jealous*

Stuck in a twisted love triangle, Jordan feels absolutely green with envy until her former best friend, Kara, introduces her to Someone even more important than Timothy.

1-57683-530-8

Torch Red: *Color Me Torn*

Zoë feels like the only virgin on the planet. But now that she's dating Justin Clark, it seems like that's about to change. Luckily, Zoë's friend Nate is there to try to save her from the biggest mistake of her life.

1-57683-531-6

Pitch Black: *Color Me Lost*

Morgan Bergstrom thinks her life is as bad as it can get, but it's about to get a whole lot worse. Her close friend Jason Harding has just killed himself, and no one knows why. As she struggles with her grief, Morgan must make her life's ultimate decision — before it's too late.

1-57683-532-4

truecolors

THINK

Burnt Orange: Color Me Wasted

Amber Conrad has a problem: Her youth group friends Simi and Lisa won't get off her case about the drinking parties she's been going to. *Everyone does it. What's the big deal?* Will she be honest with herself and her friends before things really get out of control?

1-57683-533-2

Fool's Gold: Color Me Consumed

On furlough from Papua New Guinea, Hannah Johnson spends some time with her Prada-wearing cousin Vanessa. Hannah feels like an alien around her host—everything Vanessa has is so nice. Hannah knows that stuff's not supposed to matter, but why does she feel a twinge of jealousy deep down inside?

1-57683-534-0

Blade Silver: Color Me Scarred

As Ruth Wallace attempts to stop cutting, her family life deteriorates further to the point that she isn't sure she'll ever be able to stop. Ruth needs help, but will she get it before this habit threatens her life?

1-57683-335-9

Look for the TRUECOLORS series at a Christian bookstore near you or order online at www.navpress.com.

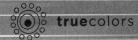
truecolors

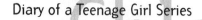

Diary of a Teenage Girl Series

Chloe

Diaries Are a Girl's Best Friend

MY NAME IS CHLOE. Chloe book one

Chloe Miller, Josh's younger sister, is a free spirit with dramatic clothes and hair. She struggles with her identity, classmates, parents, boys, and whether or not God is for real. But this unconventional high school freshman definitely doesn't hold back when she meets Him in a big, personal way. Chloe expresses God's love and grace through the girl band, Redemption, that she forms, and continues to show the world she's not willing to conform to anyone else's image of who or what she should be. Except God's, that is.
ISBN 1-59052-018-1

SOLD OUT. Chloe book two

Chloe and her fellow band members must sort out their lives as they become a hit in the local community. And after a talent scout from Nashville discovers the trio, all too soon their explosive musical ministry begins to encounter conflicts with family, so-called friends, and school. Exhilarated yet frustrated, Chloe puts her dream in God's hand and prays for Him to work out the details.
ISBN 1-59052-141-2

ROAD TRIP. Chloe book three

After signing with a major record company, Redemption's dreams are coming true. Chloe, Allie, and Laura begin their concert tour with the good-looking guys in the band Iron Cross. But as soon as the glitz and glamour wear off, the girls find life on the road a little overwhelming. Even rock-solid Laura appears to be feeling the stress—and Chloe isn't quite sure how to confront her about the growing signs of drug addiction...
ISBN 1-59052-142-0

FACE THE MUSIC. Chloe book four

Redemption has made it to the bestseller chart, but what Chloe and the girls need most is some downtime to sift through the usual high school stress with grades, friends, guys, and the prom. Chloe struggles to recover from a serious crush on the band leader of Iron Cross. Then just as an unexpected romance catches Redemption by surprise, Caitlin O'Conner—whose relationship with Josh is taking on a new dimension—joins the tour as a chaperone. Chloe's wild ride only speeds up, and this one-of-a-kind musician faces the fact that life may never be normal again.
ISBN 1-59052-241-9

Log onto www.DOATG.com